72.

RIDER ON THE
BUCKSKIN

Center Point
Large Print

Also by Peter Dawson and available from Center Point Large Print:

Willow Basin
Showdown at Anchor

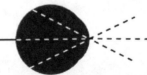

This Large Print Book carries the Seal of Approval of N.A.V.H.

RIDER ON THE BUCKSKIN

A Western Story

Peter Dawson

CENTER POINT LARGE PRINT
THORNDIKE, MAINE

ISBN: 978-1-68324-116-4 (hardcover)
ISBN: 978-1-68324-120-1 (paperback)

Library of Congress Cataloging-in-Publication Data

Names: Dawson, Peter, 1907–1957, author.
Title: Rider on the buckskin : a western story / Peter Dawson.
Description: Center Point Large Print edition. | Thorndike, Maine : Center Point Large Print, 2016.
Identifiers: LCCN 2016024186| ISBN 9781683241164 (hardcover : alk. paper) | ISBN 9781683241201 (pbk. : alk. paper)
Subjects: LCSH: Large type books. | GSAFD: Western stories.
Classification: LCC PS3507.A848 R53 2016 | DDC 813/.52—dc23
LC record available at https://lccn.loc.gov/2016024186

CHAPTER ONE

At first light this mid-October morning the heavy overcast had loosed a steady drizzle all across the range to the west of the Bear Claws. And now at 3:00 in the afternoon the misty rain still fell steadily, laying a light haze along Ute Springs' puddled streets.

Clouds hung so low along the valley that the tops of the tallest trees and the slender white spire of the church at the lower end of town were shrouded as in a settling fog. Even the brilliant golden-orange patches of cottonwood and poplar, heavily frosted this past week, did little to relieve the dull drabness of the day. And as Jim Echols stared across Sherman Street at a three-team freight hitch pulling past Rushmire's corral, noticing the way the driver sat hunched over and so plainly miserable, he shivered in sympathy with the man against the bite of the damp, chill air.

Echols had been only half listening as Lute Pleasants once again drove home the same points he had been using since the beginning of their argument. Yet now he paid a stricter attention as the man demanded: "Name me a law that says I can't put in this fence, Sheriff. Go ahead, try."

Jim Echols was weary of Pleasants's cocksure and faintly patronizing manner. Convinced that there was little point in discussing this further, he nonetheless countered: "There isn't one. Not on the books, anyway. But the law doesn't spell out how a man's to get along with his neighbors."

Lute Pleasants shook his head in much the same way as he might have had he been utterly nonplussed in trying to explain something quite simple to a child. He waited until a woman hurrying along this stretch of awninged walk had drawn on out of hearing before asking: "Why should I look out for Anchor? It's my grass Fred and Kate have been using all these years to carry them over the winter, my . . ."

"And it's their hill graze you've used every one of the four summers since you bought the Beavertail," the lawman cut in impatiently. "The same as Ruthling did before he sold you the layout. He figured it was an even swap. So did Anchor. And so did you until two weeks ago."

He glanced at Sam Cauble then, abruptly aware that Pleasants's foreman had spoken hardly a word in the ten minutes they had been standing here. "What's your idea on this fence, Cauble?"

"Mine?" Cauble smiled dourly. "I don't draw wages for havin' ideas, Sheriff. That's Lute's department."

The two Beavertail men, Echols thought, made an oddly assorted pair. Pleasants was dogmatic, assertive, while Cauble was close-mouthed, almost meek. Pleasants was fairly young—Echols guessed him to be close to his own age, thirty-two—and average height and heavy-muscled, not an ounce of fat on his big-boned frame. The Beavertail ramrod, on the other hand, was slight of stature and probably crowding fifty. And Cauble was lame, standing as crookedly right now as he usually sat a saddle.

It was perhaps this long interval of being on his bad leg that made Cauble abruptly add: "Seems we ain't gettin' much of any place hashin' this over, boss. What say we ride?"

Pleasants paid Cauble not the slightest attention as his dark eyes narrowly studied the sheriff. "This fence is a plain business proposition, money in the bank, Echols," he stated. "It's got not one damned thing to do with the Bonds. I'm just saving my grass to fatten up culls over the winter. Come the thaw next spring and I'm ditching that creek meadow so as to double my hay crop. Doesn't it all add up to plain horse sense?"

"Like hell. Not looking at it from where Kate and Fred Bond sit. They'll have to trim down their herd quick and ship heavy. And on a poor market, all because of your damned wire."

This explosive rejoinder for once caught Pleasants off balance. And as the man groped for a further point of argument, Jim Echols glanced disgustedly out onto the puddled street again, thinking that it wasn't worth it.

Idly at first, then with increasing interest, he noticed a rider on a buckskin horse leading a pack mare in on an empty tie rail at the far end of the wooden walk awning close above. The fine conformation of the buckskin was what had caught his eye and held it. He was noting the animal's high withers and powerful forequarters as Pleasants at length stubbornly insisted: "I still say I'm within my rights."

"Suppose we leave it at that, then."

Pleasants sighed gustily. "Wish you could see it my way."

Jim Echols only shrugged.

Pleasants, finally gathering that nothing was to be gained in arguing this further, abruptly said— "Let's go, Sam."—and led the way out to the two Beavertail horses tied nearby.

The lawman watched them swing out from the rail, nodding sparely in answer to Pleasants's parting lift of a hand, thinking: *His head's full of rimrock.*

In one way he felt relieved, for ever since first hearing of Beavertail's new fence he had supposed Pleasants would sooner or later want him to express an opinion on it. Well, he had made his views known. Typically he had done so in no uncertain terms. Even so he could take little satisfaction, for he saw it as having been completely futile, a waste of breath.

This session with Pleasants had left him in one

of his rare bad moods. Knowing the man only casually, he had discovered some surprising things about him—a headstrong ambition, for one, and for another a rare callousness toward range ethics. Most startling of all, though, was putting what he had learned alongside the fact that as late as the end of the summer Lute Pleasants had taken Kate Bond to several Saturday night dances at the Masonic Hall, and to the Schuster cabin raising up West Wind Valley way.

Something must have gone sour there, and, though it was strictly none of Echols's affair, he couldn't help wondering what had happened between the two to make Pleasants turn such a blind eye to the situation his fence was creating. The lawman was fond of Kate and her brother, and it rankled to see them being treated this way, their beef being so suddenly cut off from winter forage with the cold months so close at hand.

With that sobering thought he turned up the walk now, speaking in unaccustomed curtness to a passer-by, and then abruptly noticing the buckskin horse once more. The animal was tied alongside the pack mare at the rail up ahead. Its rider had disappeared, probably into one of the neighboring stores, having thrown his patched yellow slicker across the saddle to keep it dry. Now that the saddle was empty, the buckskin looked even bigger than at first glance. And Echols, really impressed, all but forgot his ill humor as he forsook the shelter of the awning to step out into the mud and stand alongside the horse, head tilted against the raw slant of the rain.

"You're a proud-lookin' devil," he muttered admiringly, running a hand over the wet, rippling muscles along the buckskin's shoulder, feeling the flesh quiver at the touch of his hand, then relax.

He liked the way the horse's ears stood so sharply forward, the mark of good breeding in the small head. He began wondering if he could buy the animal, and a small excitement lifted in him.

Then all at once he was noticing the buckskin's jaw brand, a Half Moon, and trying to place it, for it was a brand strange to this country, yet one familiar to him. Suddenly he did remember where he had heard of it and his hawkish face went slack with surprise. And in that fraction of a second the past minute's enjoyment ended for him; he was once again in the same foul mood he'd been in on parting from Pleasants. Only this time his temper flared for a far different reason.

He looked quickly around, scanning the walk in both directions, his interest in the buckskin's owner sharpening. He stepped back under the rail to the walk and dipped his head to let the water run from the trough of his hat.

He was standing there some three minutes later when a tall, rangy man carrying a half-filled gunny sack appeared out of Dendahl's Emporium two doors below and came toward him along the walk,

10

small-rowelled spurs whispering metallically at each stride.

It had become Jim Echols's habit over his three years in office to take notice of strangers passing through the country. Yet rarely had he sized one up as carefully, or as scornfully, as he did this one.

The stranger wore a cowhide coat a trifle too small for his wide span of shoulder. He was smoking a pipe and he was young—the lawman put him in his middle twenties—with a lean and sun-darkened face shadowed by several days of razor neglect. Contrasting strongly with that deeply tanned skin was a pair of deep-set and alert blue eyes.

So this is him, Echols was thinking scornfully as the stranger approached. *Not many of 'em darken down so soon after they're out.*

Noticing that his stare was being returned now, the sheriff's irritation became even stronger than it had been while he waited. And it was because of his ill humor, plus the fact that under any circumstances he wouldn't have wasted his time being polite to this man, that he bluntly stated: "You must be Frank Rivers."

The other halted two strides away, surprise washing over his angular features as he reached up to take the pipe from his mouth. Then, unexpectedly, he was smiling.

"So I am," he drawled good-naturedly. "But where've I seen you before?"

"You haven't." The lawman caught no visible reaction in the man and tonelessly added: "Maybe it'd help if you knew my name. It's Jim Echols."

"Oh." A definite reserve, a flintiness, settled across this Frank Rivers's face. "Some relation of Bill Echols?"

"Bill's my cousin."

Rivers shrugged sparely. "So you know all about it."

"I damned well do." Derisively Echols asked: "Hasn't been too long since the governor pardoned you, has it?"

"Four months."

The sheriff just now happened to notice the end of a tied-down holster hanging below the line of Rivers's coat. Nodding down to it, he tartly commented: "Didn't know you were allowed to pack a gun."

The taller man deliberately, coolly measured Echols all the way from hat to boots before saying: "It was a full pardon, Echols, not a parole."

That deceptively soft drawl belied the steel behind the words. And before the sheriff had a chance to say anything, Rivers lowered the gunny sack to the walk planks, pocketed his pipe, and just as quietly added: "It appears you've got a chip on your shoulder, friend. Are you asking me to knock it off?"

Jim Echols started momentarily, left wordless, and he grudgingly wondered just then how bad a licking he or almost any other man would take if he chose to accept such a bald invitation as this. Rivers was big and had a look of rawhide toughness about him. And, now that he noticed it, the sheriff could see that Rivers's clean-lined face bore marks of violence, marks probably left there by the man's having survived the countless brawls of better than four years in the territorial prison. What might once have been an aquiline nose was slightly crooked and flattened, and the pale two-inch line of a scar showed through the wavy black hair over his left temple.

But what galled Echols the most was this man's coolness and sureness, the almost good-natured yet deadly serious way he had spoken. Echols judged him to be quite capable of taking care of himself either with fists or with a gun, though that wasn't the lawman's reason for now remarking: "Better watch your step, Rivers. You're talking to the sheriff."

"So?" Frank Rivers seemed only faintly surprised and not at all impressed. "Well, now that you've looked me over, is there anything else you'd like to know?"

"One thing." There was no tolerance whatsoever in Echols for this man and his tone was larded with contempt as he queried: "You're still on the prowl for that pair? The men you say held up the stage and killed your father while they crippled Bill?"

"And framed me. Yes."

The lawman smiled crookedly. "One was lame, wasn't he?"

"Lame and a drunk. A carpenter."

"Having any luck locating him?"

Rivers overlooked the biting sarcasm. "Not any . . . yet."

"I can save you some time. The only lame man around here was talking with me right here when you rode in. Name of Sam Cauble. And he's no carpenter."

"So I just found out in that store back there."

The lawman's feelings toward Rivers had mellowed not at all, and now he gave vent to them by recklessly observing: "If I'd cooked up the story you gave at your trial, I'd maybe do the same as you're doin'. Sashay around a few months letting on like I was hunting these two men, that lame one and his partner. I'd do it just to make the governor's pardon look good."

Rivers eyed the sheriff with a faint though patently genuine amusement. "I get a combing over like this every now and then. So go ahead, throw in the spurs."

Jim Echols's thin face tightened and reddened. "They've rigged up a chair for Bill with wheels on it. He spends his time in the chair and in bed. It's been five years. He'll never walk again."

His voice grating with fury, the lawman was crowded into rashly asking: "Just how much of the gold you got off that stage did you hand over to that man to lie you out of prison?"

"Have your fun," Rivers drawled easily, though his face had lost a shade of color.

Quite suddenly Jim Echols had had enough of this. "You're not wanted around here, Rivers," he said in a voice trembling and dry with indignation. "Get on that horse, hit the county line, and keep on going."

"So I'd planned."

Frank Rivers reached down now to lift the gunny sack from the walk. He stepped on past Echols and, ignoring him completely, went on out to the buckskin.

The lawman said loudly: "I meant that. Keep clear of this county."

Rivers was pulling on his slicker and glanced around. "Bend's over the county line, isn't it? That's where I'm headed, north and over the pass."

"North? East you mean. There's a new fence closing off the pass trail. You'll have to go around by way of the road."

Rivers swung up into the saddle before dryly stating: "Found out about that, too. Only I'm told a man can ride around the end of the fence. So I'll take the pass trail."

He turned the buckskin away then, the pack mare following. And Jim Echols, watching him head out onto the mired street, glared at his broad back with a look of scalding dislike.

CHAPTER TWO

The road running north from Ute Springs followed the winding, brushy creek bottom for the first four miles. And over much of that distance Lute Pleasants was thinking back on his talk with Jim Echols, trying to weigh the impression he felt he'd made on the man.

Finally he decided that it didn't really matter. The main point their argument had proven was that Echols could and would do nothing about the fence. This in itself was so comforting that Pleasants could now dismiss all thought of any interference on the part of the law, something he hadn't been at all sure of until this afternoon.

Things were working out about as he had supposed they would, even better perhaps, and the prospect of what the next year might bring was nice to think about. Because of that he wasn't minding this raw, rainy afternoon at all. The earlier the winter, the better it suited his plans. Never had he felt more confident of the future.

Just now a sound, a whistling from overhead, intruded upon his reflections. He looked up in time to see a wedge of ducks circle low under the gray clouds in the direction of the creek, wheel, set their wings, and drop from sight beyond the brilliant yellow-orange background

16

of the cottonwoods and willows up ahead. *They're early this year,* he told himself, seeing this sign of winter's premature arrival as a good omen.

His mare had been lagging, and he dug her sharply in the barrel with spurs to bring her up alongside Sam Cauble's gray, heavy-handed on the reins as always. He glanced around at Cauble, who sat canted over in the saddle favoring his game leg. Sam looked cold and miserable, his thin face pinched, sallow. He rode with chin almost touching the wet front of his canvas coat that was stiff from the cold and its heavy coating of brown paint.

Cauble, having nicely restrained himself in town, was, as usual, drinking. And, as usual, he appeared to be drinking just enough to keep himself sealed off in his own private world. That had been the way with the man these many years. Whiskey, good or bad, was as necessary to him as food. With it he deadened the pain of his bad leg and quieted an uneasy conscience.

Just now he stirred, as he had every half mile or so since leaving town, and reached into the pouch of his saddle for the flat stoneware quart bottle he always carried. He looked around, found Pleasants watching him, and offered the bottle.

Pleasants only shook his head, eyeing him wryly and with a faint amusement. So Cauble drank, dropped the bottle back into the pouch, and settled into his slouch again.

"You look beat up, Sam," Pleasants commented. "Cold and shriveled. Better take another pull."

Cauble lifted his head and eyed Pleasants sourly a moment. "I can handle the cold right enough. But there's other things I can't."

"Such as what?"

Cauble's eyes mirrored a faint anger then as, reaching up with a forefinger to trowel the wet from both sides of his bristling moustache, he queried: "Think Echols swallowed your fancy story?"

Abruptly Pleasants realized that this man, ordinarily mild of manner, was in an unaccountably ugly mood. "Better do like I said, take another nip and wash the sand out of your craw."

The other shook his head. "Won't help." With unexpected vehemence he burst out: "Damn it, Lute, I'm scared! Scared clean down into my bones."

Pleasants was genuinely puzzled. "Scared of what?"

"Of you! Of your having gone so hog greedy with this fence." Cauble laughed loudly, mockingly. "You and your savin' all this grass for feedin' culls."

Lute Pleasants's square face took on a chill look. "Suppose you let me do the thinking for the both of us."

"That's the trouble, you been doin' it all. And your thinkin's wrong, dead wrong." When

Pleasants had nothing to say, Cauble went on in abrupt seriousness. "Lean back and take a long look at your hole card, Lute. Look back five years. You came here with our money and bought Beavertail for a song. Six months later I drifted in, a plumb total stranger, and hired on with the crew. We rigged it so even the Lord himself couldn't guess we're brothers. We been saltin' away . . ."

"Half-brothers, Sam. The old woman married a good man after she got rid of your father."

Cauble decided to overlook the slur and said quietly, still seriously: "We've had it good. As soft a spot as two strays like us could dream of havin'. For the first time in ten years we're livin' under our right names and sleepin' easy nights, with not a soul wise to who we really are. Now you get it in your hard head to risk the whole caboodle on a fool gamble."

"But it isn't a gamble." Pleasants, whose thoughts ran straight and clear on this matter, wondered why he was bothering to argue. "We'll make money, a stack of it."

"What's wrong with the way it's been till now? With the way it was for twenty years between Anchor and Beavertail? With both outfits using our creek meadows for winter graze, and both summerin' high on Anchor range?"

Lute Pleasants sighed impatiently. "Look, Sam. We're not related to the Bonds like old Ruthling was. So it isn't up to us to give Anchor more than

19

we get back. Like I told Echols, it's a plain business proposition to put in this fence and ditch the creek bottom."

"It's no plain business proposition to turn your neighbors against you," Cauble retorted acidly. "This fence'll about finish Anchor and you damn' well know it. Then there's this other," he went on, giving Pleasants no chance to interrupt. "This loco notion of yours to sneak in some night and dig out our bed of the creek up there on Anchor where she splits to feed both layouts. Hell, man, they could easy find out about that even if you wait till the freeze. Then you'd have Echols on your neck for stealin' water."

Pleasants's sloping shoulders lifted wearily. "I've gone over it with you at least ten times and damned if I do again. Only I still say that with the fence and the new ditches we'll make about double what we have each year so far."

The man's cool and precise tone, his cocksureness, only stirred Cauble's rancor to a higher pitch. And now the older man was prodded to rashness as he dryly pronounced: "Beats me how you nurse a grudge. You'd never in this world have thought of the fence, of wirin' Anchor off in the hills, if Kate Bond hadn't turned the cold shoulder to your courtin' her. If she hadn't . . ."

Suddenly, so fast it was hard to see his hand moving, Lute Pleasants reached over, snatched a hold on the front of Cauble's coat, and nearly hauled him from the gray's back. He struck his half-brother two vicious, open-handed blows across the face, tilting the other's head around. Then, as the gray shied, he shoved Cauble away so roughly that the older man almost fell from the far side of the saddle.

"Any more talk like that and I'll beat your head flat!"

There was a wicked, killing light in Pleasants's dark eyes. Cauble noticed that and was nonetheless furious beyond caring as he reached up and wiped away the blood already staining his mustache at one corner of his mouth. His move had drawn Pleasants's attention from his other hand. And now that hand all at once lifted into view from his far side, fisting his .45.

He reined hard away from Pleasants, laid the gun across the swell of his saddle, and hoarsely burst out: "It's been about two years since you belted me like that. The last time you was told I'd never take it again. Now open your big hairy ears and take in what I got to say."

Their animals had come to a stand. And Lute Pleasants, warned by the other's half-crazed look, was careful to keep his hands folded on the horn of the saddle. Sam Cauble was too enraged, and perhaps too far gone with drink, to be trusted with his finger on the trigger.

So now Pleasants's tone was mild as he said: "Just plain forgot myself, Sam. Put that away and . . ."

"Like hell! I said to sit there and listen, and you'll damn' well do it! Think back. Remember? Remember who held the horses that night five years ago and saw it all happen? Remember who used the shotgun and then gun-whipped the driver and came close to kickin' his guts loose?"

"Careful."

"Me be careful? It's you that could be in hot water, hot to boilin', not me."

"If you ever breathe so much as a word about that night . . ."

"Now we're gettin' somewhere," Cauble cut in, his thin lips tight in a derisive smile. "You begin to remember I cut some ice in this pond after all."

Pleasants was thinking: *Stall him, cool him down.* Aloud he drawled: "Say the word and I'll buy you out, Sam. You can pack up your tools and pull out any day you say."

"And go back to mendin' gates and trimmin' windows like any other busted-down carpenter, eh?" the other came back at him, his breathing laying a misty vapor before his thin face. "Suppose I did? Suppose I up and took off. Disappeared, took on another name. Then I could write a certain party up north, couldn't I? Party by the name of Rivers."

He saw Lute Pleasants's face lose its ruddiness and blanch with fury. He was taking grim satisfaction in that as he went on: "So we got that squared away. I could see you swingin' by the

22

neck if I wanted. Sort of hauls you up short to think I'm still half this partnership, don't it? Well, Lute boy, from now on in I have a say in what we do."

Pleasants's wary glance dropped to Cauble's gun, seeing it still lined at his middle. He had barely enough grip on himself to realize that either because of the whiskey or out of sheer desperation Sam Cauble was right now very, very dangerous. So he sat rock-solid in the saddle, saying lamely: "You've always had a say in what we've done."

"Not by a long shot. I claimed in the beginning this fence was a mistake. That was because of Echols, because we'd had the bad luck to settle near the cousin of the man you beat so bad that night. Well, I got soft in the head and let you persuade me Echols could never tie us in with that other, even if he did work up a grudge against us. But now, Lute boy, that's over with."

"What does that mean . . . over with?"

"On the way in you were tellin' me how you're goin' to give Phil Crowe that leftover wire, so he can string the fence on across his place as far as the breaks. Wire Anchor up there tight in the hills, you said. With not enough feed and no way out except to drive their beef sixty miles east over the peaks. And with winter coming on you allowed they'd never make it."

"That's the general idea," Pleasants admitted grudgingly.

"Crowe, you said, would take the bait because of that rustlin' charge old Bond brought against him before he died years back." Pausing, Cauble hefted the Colt menacingly. "Crowe's just a sour enough old coot to throw in with you and shut Anchor out of the valley. But you know what? You ain't even going to put the proposition to Crowe. Know why? Because your partner says it's a risky, fool thing to do. We keep our fence, but we don't sell Crowe the notion of stringin' one."

Pleasants was held mute by rage and contempt. His thoughts must have mirrored themselves on his face, for in another moment Cauble was telling him: "Right now you'd give your left arm to pull out my windpipe. All right, stew in your damn' bile. But when you've cooled down tonight, you'll see how right I am. I say to let things be like they are. We can give this feeder business a try. But you'll forget draggin' Anchor down to ruin so you can buy the outfit cheap, like you been plannin'."

"Who said that's what I planned?"

"I say so. I know you like . . . like I do the feel of this here Forty-Five."

Cauble let the words sink in. Then, seeing Pleasants about to speak, he added hurriedly: "I been totin' most of the weight around here lately, don't forget. Livin' up there in that patched-up tent at the fence camp, bossin' those three hard-cases you hired. Tonight, for a sample, I ride that wire from midnight on. In this foul weather. Just because of your harebrained notion that Anchor'll sooner or later try and cut fence on us. All right, I'll go along on that. But when this fence is finished come the end of the week, I'm movin' on down to the layout to start fixin' up the wagon shed like I did the porch last summer. I'll sleep inside and eat grub that don't rot the belly out of a goat."

Pleasants waited, wanting to be certain that Cauble had finished. When he was sure, he said tonelessly: "You've got a lot off your chest, Sam. Too much maybe."

"Time I got it off." The lame man pointed down the road ahead with the .45. "Trot along now. And keep those hands restin' right easy where they are."

Pleasants grudgingly prodded the mare with spurs and she started on. She had carried him a good two hundred yards before he caught the muffled pound of Sam Cauble's gray sounding from behind him. Looking around, he saw Cauble cutting from the road toward the mouth of a shallow draw in the creek bluff.

The dam that had been holding his temper in check burst then, and he cursed obscenely at not having thought to tie a rifle to his saddle for this ride into town today. Going on, his thoughts seething, he presently followed the road as it swung away from the creek through thickets of chokeberry and hawthorn, glistening with the rain.

Then shortly he was traveling up the long grade of the creek bluff, in less than a minute enveloped in a light fog that deadened the hoof falls of the mare as she made higher ground.

By the time the road's puddled ruts had leveled out across the grassy bench above, Pleasants's thinking was coming a little straighter. Ordinarily he was a man to hold a tight rein on his emotions; he was a cool and heady thinker. But this run-in with Sam had been too personal, had rubbed raw too many old sore spots for him not to feel it strongly and be deeply embittered by it.

He saw Sam as being wrong on every point. The man was stone blind not to see the opportunity staring them in the face. Looking back across the years, he could pick out other times when his half-brother had interfered, when he'd been too faint-hearted. Sam had become a real liability, his appetite for drink alone meaning there was perpetually great risk in trusting him.

Just now the man's blunt and deadly earnest threat of betraying him loomed high over all their other differences, made them seem almost petty. Sam Cauble had, as he had bragged, the power to destroy him.

A premature dusk was thickening the light around Beavertail's drab clutter of pens and outbuildings when Pleasants turned the mare into the barn corral and walked on over to the gray-weathered frame house. The air had turned colder and a few fluffy flakes of snow were beginning to drift down out of the leaden sky.

The cook was the only other man on the place. He had finished an early supper, so Pleasants ate alone at the table in the kitchen, brooding all the while on how he was to deal with Cauble. Only once did he speak to the cook.

"Charlie, you keep salting this mush so heavy and I'll wash your face with the next batch."

"You want new cook, you go to hell and look for him," was the Chinaman's placid answer.

Later, after Charlie had gone to the bunkhouse taking the dogs with him, Pleasants sat in the room across the hallway that served him as both office and bedroom, wondering if there was any way at all of making his peace with Sam Cauble. Presently and with a stark and somehow pleasing finality he knew that there wasn't.

He made his decision then, made it unalterably and without emotion, and was afterward genuinely amazed to think that he hadn't arrived at it years ago.

Lute Pleasants had the unique faculty of never doubting himself, and of rarely worrying once he had made up his mind to something. It was that way with him now. Knowing how he was to deal with this situation, he reached over, turned down the lamp, and blew it out, slumped down more comfortably in the barrel chair alongside his desk, and in two more minutes was fast asleep.

When he wakened, at once alert and refreshed, the room was chill, the isinglass window of the stove in the near corner glowing a dull cherry red. He came erect and struck a match to see the hands of the clock over the desk naming the hour to be 1:10 a.m., which was quite satisfactory.

An hour and twenty minutes later he was riding a roan gelding up the last climbing reach of a shallow timbered coulée high in the hills toward the line of his new fence, knowing exactly where he was. A faint moon glow shone through the overcast to reveal objects at perhaps a hundred-foot distance. The ground was ankle-deep with snow and more was falling steadily out of the blackness overhead.

The chuck wagon and tent of his fence camp, he knew, were half a mile to the north of this point. Better than a mile southward, and higher in the hills, Anchor's headquarters sprawled across the center of a broad, lush-grassed park rimmed by spruce and aspen.

Pleasants came out of the saddle when he reached the fence, eyeing the ground to this side of the two nearest posts. No shadow of hoof prints disturbed the smooth surface of the snow, telling him that Sam Cauble hadn't yet ridden this way.

He took a pair of wire-cutters from a coat pocket now and stepped over to the fence, deliberately cutting the three tight strands of barb wire that sang and whipped away as he made the cuts, rolling in on the posts to either side.

Leading his horse southward along the fence, he made four more cuts, then swung clumsily up into the saddle once more, afterward looking off to the north in the direction from which he expected Sam Cauble would be coming. He heard nothing, saw nothing moving against the blackness, and shortly put the roan through the cut fence and lined out in the direction of Anchor.

He'll think . . . Lute was right after all, and come stormin' along primed for bear. He laughed softly in his absolute certainty that Cauble, when he rode along here, would notice the breaks in the fence and try following him without wasting the time to backtrack him.

He had ridden on for several hundred yards when, rounding a clump of pines, he all at once saw a pale glow of firelight reflected from the snowy slope of a timber-capped ridge directly ahead. Reining in instantly, puzzled and wary, he tried to understand the meaning of the fire. Then abruptly he thought he knew.

The old pass trail, all but abandoned now with the improved road crossing a lower pass to Bend on the far side of the Bear Claws, crossed the line of his fence at a padlocked gate that was less than a quarter of a mile to the south. It was more than likely that someone riding the trail had rounded the end of the fence and was camped above.

This notion had barely firmed in his mind when, from not too far behind him, the gusty whickering of a horse suddenly shattered the night's stillness. He instantly pulled the roan hard to the left and headed up a slope that shortly brought him to the margin of the pines.

He slid quickly aground, roughly shortening his hold on the reins and clamping a hand about the roan's nose as he used the other to draw his heavy rifle from the saddle's scabbard.

In ten more seconds he made out a faint moving shadow below that gradually took on the shape of a horse and rider. As he watched, the man below pulled his animal to a stand.

Pleasants dropped the reins and lifted the rifle. This Winchester was his favorite weapon, a .45-75, heavier than the popular .44-40 and of seldom-seen caliber. It was deadly accurate. And now, knowing it so well, he lined it at the horseman below with a fierce exultancy rising in him at the certainty that this had to be his half-brother and that Sam was as good as dead.

But that instant his target began moving again, slanting off across the foot of the slope. Then, almost before he realized what was happening, the night had swallowed that indistinct shape.

With unruly impatience Pleasants climbed into the saddle once more and headed the roan obliquely across the slope through the trees, abruptly swinging higher as it suddenly occurred to him what Sam was doing.

Sam had seen the fire up ahead. He must now be thinking that the man who had cut the fence was responsible for the fire. He would be riding straight for it, no longer interested in the tracks he had followed to this point.

The fire, Pleasants was thinking, would make it easier to be certain of where he placed his bullet.

CHAPTER THREE

Frank Rivers could scarcely believe what he was hearing, or what he was seeing. He had been up out of his blankets arranging the three keeper logs of the fire to last out the remaining hours of the night when this mustached, furious stranger rode in unannounced out of the snow blackness, sitting the saddle crookedly, and a rifle leveled across saddle.

Now, trying to make sense of the tongue-lashing the man had just given him, Rivers protested: "All I did to your fence was ride around the end of it. If you . . ."

"Hogwash!" the other cut in venomously. "You're an Anchor hand and you damn' well did cut our wire! Now you'll throw your hull onto one of those nags and come along with . . ."

The thunderclap explosion of a heavy rifle burst across the night from behind Rivers. He saw the stranger's slight frame pounded back and off balance. For one split second he stood rooted in a paralysis of surprise, watching the man's thin face tighten in agony, seeing him sway loosely in the saddle as the gray nervously side-stepped. Then, suddenly aware of his own danger, he wheeled and lunged into the shadows beyond reach of the fire's light.

He threw himself into the snow and rolled beneath the low branches of a spruce, wriggled in close to the tree's broad base. A brief glance toward the fire showed him the gray standing with trailing reins, the stranger lying, sprawled and motionless, in the snow.

The night's absolute hush possessed an explosive quality that made him shallow his breathing, straining to catch the slightest stray sound that would bring warning of the killer stalking him. He had waited out a long quarter minute when suddenly the stillness was broken by the muffled hoof pound of a hard-ridden horse sounding from up the trail.

His long frame stiffened, and in that instant he felt even more trapped and helpless than he had while staring into the bore of the stranger's rifle, for his holstered .44 and rifle lay beneath the saddle at the head of his blankets beyond the fire.

But in three more seconds he abruptly realized that the sound was fading instead of gathering strength, and he breathed a long whistling sigh of relief. Yet he didn't move until the night had swallowed the last remote echo of that horse running into the upcountry distance. And even after he had crawled out and was on his feet again, his nerves stayed taut and every sense in him was keened to a hard alertness.

He warily made a circle of the fire, keeping well back in the shadows, then knelt by his blankets to pull the .44 from beneath his saddle and buckled it about his waist. Afterward he strode quickly in on the fire, his brief glance down at the stranger met by the glazed stare of wide-open eyes. He wheeled away at once and hurried to drag the carefully arranged logs from the blaze, knowing without any doubt that the man was dead.

He strode on out to the gray as the glowing log ends hissed against the snow. Leading the animal well out of the light, he tied the reins to an aspen, then loosened the cinch. It was then that the sudden letdown made him start trembling, every nerve in him raw from the punishment of these past five minutes.

"Now what?"

His voice laid an alien, startling sound across the night's absolute hush. He could supply no answer to the question beyond knowing that these past minutes had made a marked man of him. Thinking this, wondering what he should do next, he walked on across to the fire and by its feeble glow looked at his watch and saw that it lacked twenty minutes of being 4:00 a.m.

He had a choice to make here and now. He could throw saddles on the buckskin and mare and head up the trail, counting on the feeble moonlight to let him find his way over the pass. By first light he would be long gone, his tracks snowed over, leaving behind him the mystery of a killing that might not even be discovered for a day or two.

Yet a subtle resentment over the way the stranger had died presently began to undermine this too easy line of reasoning. He went across to light his pipe and hunker down beside his blankets in the shelter of a pine, remembering that his father had died in much the same way this stranger had. And, though he and his parent had disagreed violently on many things, he could still feel a trace of the fury that had held him on learning that a charge of buckshot in the back had snuffed out George Rivers's life.

Finally he knew that he had no choice but that of packing the body back down to Ute Springs once it got light. His instinct was to trust Jim Echols's sense of fairness even though the man obviously loathed him and believed him to be guilty of having killed his father, of having nearly beat Bill Echols to death, and finally of having bought his way out of prison.

But, Rivers reasoned, so had other good men been blind to his claim of innocence over the past five years. Thinking back on his meeting with the sheriff he could recall nothing to indicate that Echols wouldn't be fair and honest in dealing with this situation, especially if he voluntarily gave himself up and offered what evidence he had.

It mattered a great deal to Rivers just now that nothing should stop him in his hunt for the two men who had held up the stage that night almost five years ago. If he should risk turning his back on this murder, there was a strong likelihood that he might eventually be blamed for it.

When at last the new day dawned, it came weakly, with snow still settling steadily over the gold and emerald sweep of aspen and spruce forest shrouding the high shoulders below the peaks of the Bear Claws. An hour later a thin twilight still lay along this stretch of trail as Rivers finished saddling the mare and buckskin, picketed them once more on the slope close below, and came back to his fire.

In spite of the thickly falling snow and the poor light he heated some water, got out his razor and a shard of mirror, and spent ten minutes over a careful shave, having instinctively sensed that his looking like a saddle tramp might count against him today whereas his appearance didn't ordinarily matter one way or the other.

Afterward he led the gray over to the canvas-shrouded shape near the fire and managed awkwardly to heave the dead man across the saddle. He roped the gelding's awkward burden securely, and was tying the last knots when he happened to glance around to find both the buckskin and the mare standing alert, ears forward, looking up the draw.

He wheeled. A rider was watching him from a point where the pines heavily shadowed the upper trail some fifty yards distant.

Rivers dropped the rope end, letting hand settle

against the cold bone handle of the .44. And for the space of several seconds he could feel the other's glance warily studying him across the snow-hazed interval separating them.

All at once his visitor called: "Who've you got there . . . Sam Cauble?"

The voice jolted him with a hard surprise, for it was a woman's. It took him a deliberate interval to put down his astonishment and answer: "You'll have to tell me who he is."

Seconds passed, both of them remaining motionless. Rivers had almost decided that the woman was about to turn and ride away. Then, again surprising him, she brought her sorrel straight down toward the fire.

She drew rein a scant twenty feet short of him, and he saw that she was young. She wore a heavy maroon wool coat and a pair of man's waist overalls. Her face, fair and reddened by the cold, held an odd quality of both delicacy and strength. Her hair was a deep mahogany chestnut and she wore it knotted at the nape of her neck, its folds held by a big silver clasp. Striking she was, yet the most striking thing about her was her eyes, a greenish hazel.

They were very bright and alive now in the faintly nervous way they regarded him. She glanced briefly at the dead man, saying: "You'd be twenty miles from here if you'd done this. We heard the shot across at the house, which is why

I'm here." Hesitating momentarily, she asked: "Who did kill Cauble?"

Frank Rivers was taken aback by the quickness with which this girl had evidently made up her mind to trust him. There was a quality of high-spiritedness and directness about her that demanded the same in return, so that he told her: "If you heard the shot, you can understand why I didn't get a look at whoever it was." He lifted an arm, pointing up the trail. "He cut this man down from off there, the way you rode in."

"How does it happen Cauble was up here?"

"He drifted in while I was stirring around, building up the fire, made some wild talk about how I'd cut that fence down below. About me working for some outfit that'd like to see the wire down."

The girl's expression turned instantly grave. "Then he thought you were working for me. This is our range . . . Anchor's."

"That's the brand he named."

"You were just traveling the trail, on your way through?"

"I was." Rivers's eyes took on a wry glint. "Now I'm headed back down to take the poor devil to town. No use skipping out on . . ."

His words broke off as a sharp ringing sound shuttled up from below, a sound he recognized as the striking of a shod hoof against rock. Half turning, he looked below along the trail and made out the indistinct shapes of three riders trotting their horses in this direction through the light fog of settling snow.

"You may be wishing you hadn't waited around." The girl had followed his glance, and, as she made this pronouncement, there was no warmth whatsoever in her tone. "These are Cauble's friends," she added.

"Not yours, I take it."

"No." Over a brief pause, she told him: "Lute Pleasants is the one in the lead. He'll do the talking. Sometimes he doesn't think before he lets his tongue go. So don't let him crowd you into doing anything foolish."

Rivers sighed resignedly, finding nothing in her words to give him comfort. The riders had slowed their pace now and were peering in this direction, and he knew that they had seen his fire. Then in a few more seconds one man cut away and angled up the brushy slope toward a margin of pines at a higher elevation than this stretch of trail. And Rivers, watching the other two come on again, saw something ominous in this dividing of their forces.

"Maybe you'd better move along, miss," he said.

The girl gave him a brief, wondering glance that held a quality of undisguised respect. "Certainly not. You'll need me."

By now the two riders were close enough below

for Rivers to catch the creak of saddle leather and the jingle of their spurs and bridle chains. From above, the third man's horse abruptly set up a racket, pushing through a patch of scrub oak, the sound telling Rivers that they had nicely contrived to put him and the girl between them.

It was the man who had been pointed out to him as Lute Pleasants who led his companion up the last gentle climb and reined in directly beyond the fire some twenty yards away. Pleasants's square, ruddy face set belligerently as his quick glance went to the gray, shifted briefly to Rivers, and finally settled on the girl.

"Didn't know you'd hired a killer, Kate," he said tonelessly.

"I'd never seen this man until five minutes . . ."

An angry, slashing gesture of Pleasants's free hand cut the girl's words short. "Let's have no guff about this. The boys heard the shot, got spooky, and started looking for Sam. Found your cuts in the fence and Sam gone. So they sent a man across to rout me out. Now this!"

Pleasants tilted his head toward the gray, and his glance swung hard on Rivers. "Didn't give you time to pull out, did we? What were you aimin' to do, pack him up onto the pass and cave in a cutbank on him?"

"No. I was taking him down to the sheriff."

Rivers's quiet tone seemed to rouse Pleasants to a higher pitch of fury. For all at once he looked

40

beyond Rivers and said in a clipped, brittle voice: "Draw a bead on the middle of his back, Harry!"

"Lute, stop this!" the girl cried in a hushed, frightened way. "Let him explain!"

As she spoke, Rivers made an abrupt half turn to find the man behind him sitting his horse at about the same distance from him as Pleasants. This one had already reached down to his rifle and half drawn it from its sheath. But now he suddenly froze, motionless.

He had been watching Rivers closely. This instant he had seen Rivers's high frame bend slightly and go rigid, with right hand lifting sparely to within finger spread of his holster. There was a smoky, challenging light in Rivers's blue eyes, and the man was shocked and warned by it.

Lute Pleasants also caught that startling change in Rivers, as did his crewman alongside him. Pleasants's outraged expression thinned now before one of slow-breaking wonderment. It was as though some unforeseen element had all at once thrust itself into this situation, an element Pleasants didn't quite know how to deal with.

Frank Rivers noticed this indecision in the man and let the seconds run on and the tension build against these three, warily waiting for one of them to make the slightest move. He had all three barely within the limits of his vision, the single man hard to his left, the other two obliquely to his right.

And with the certainty that they hadn't quite

managed to box him in between them, that they were momentarily unsure of themselves, a feeling of wild recklessness ran through him, making him softly say: "Let's get on with it."

CHAPTER FOUR

Frank Rivers's flat challenge, thrown so unexpectedly at Pleasants and his two crewmen, faded across the snowy stillness. And for a long moment not one of these four men so much as let an eyelid fall in the face of this threat of exploding violence.

It was Rivers who finally moved, taking four deliberate backward steps that heightened the odds in his favor. For, as he halted, he was no longer positioned between them, and could nicely see all three men at the same time. And, much to his relief, his move had put more distance between him and the girl.

He could still feel the pressure they were putting on him, and he knew with a grim finality that they were waiting for only the slightest break in his sureness to use as an excuse for shooting him down. At the moment they were wary, uncertain of him. But this would last only as long as he made it last.

So now he drawled—"Who wants to give it a try?"—and stood as he had been, wide shoulders hunched slightly forward, right hand hanging close to the .44 Colt.

It was Harry, the man Lute Peasants had some

moments ago invited to draw a bead on Rivers's back with his rifle, whose nerve was the first to give way.

"Not me, stranger." He made an expansive gesture of letting go his grip on the rifle and folding hands across the horn of his saddle.

Rivers's glance shuttled squarely on Pleasants now, his eyes flinty, faintly contemptuous in the regard they put on the man. "You do a lot of talking, neighbor. Got anything to back it up?"

Pleasants was jarred by a harder surprise, and over the next brief interval he evidently weighed his chances and saw them as less than even. For without preliminary he all at once said: "Ben, go get Sam and we'll be on our way."

The man alongside him turned his horse across to the gray and leaned down to gather up the reins, and in that moment Frank Rivers knew that the worst of this was over for him. Harry now came down and joined Pleasants, circling Rivers at a respectful distance, and finally they were all three together as Ben led the gray across.

It was typical of Lute Pleasants that he should try and have the last word in this affair. He had been humbled, out-guessed, and now he showed how all this rankled as he pointedly ignored Rivers and eyed the girl. "Two hours from now there'll be a warrant out for this man, Kate. Maybe one out for you, too. I'll see . . ."

"More talk," Rivers's deceptively soft drawl cut

him short. "Man, if you've got any horse sense at all, you'll move along."

For an instant Rivers thought he had crowded Pleasants too far, for the man's dark eyes smoldered with a furious, killing light and it appeared that he was letting anger override his sense of caution. But even then it seemed he was taking into account what the last half minute had shown him of this tall stranger.

Abruptly hauling his horse around, Pleasants led his men away without a further word. And the girl, hearing Rivers breathe a soft, whistling sigh of relief, looked around at him and was startled to see him slowly shake his head, and then reach up to push his hat back and run a hand across his damp forehead.

He intercepted her puzzled look. "Lucky, eh?"

Her puzzlement became stronger. "You . . . you were . . . ?"

"Scared? Sure, weren't you?"

"But I was sure. . . . The way you stood up to them and . . ."

Whatever her thought had been she didn't complete it. And Rivers, half understanding, told her: "When you're down to only a few chips, you bet like you had a pocketful."

The utter lack of pretense in this man confounded Kate Bond. He was a different person now from the one he had been a minute ago. His manner was gentle, his words soft-spoken once

45

more. And suddenly, unaccountably, a feeling of warmth and friendliness toward him made her smile down at him and say: "Lute Pleasants will never know that, will he? He'll turn it over in that sharp mind of his. He'll wonder what would have happened if he'd made his try at you. He'll never forgive himself for not knowing the answer."

She had never before been a witness to such a tense, ominous situation, and now its aftereffects made her momentarily lose grip on her emotions. She began laughing uncontrollably. But then the startled, worried look that came to Rivers's eyes sobered and embarrassed her.

"Forgive me for acting like a twelve-year-old. But if anything had happened to you, it would have been because of me, because of Anchor."

"Well, it didn't happen, which is all that matters."

There was a steadiness and a good-naturedness about this man that was like a tonic to Kate Bond now. And in genuine gratefulness she impulsively asked: "Is there anything at all I can do to help? I know this country above as well as I know the yard at the house. If you're . . ."

His expression underwent a change as she spoke. He was frowning, avoiding her glance.

She asked: "What is it?"

Rivers seemed all at once ill at ease. He stooped and tossed several lengths of wood onto the fire, and afterward peered down the trail as though studying Pleasants and the two others who were now but faint blurred shadows behind the hazy curtain of the falling snow.

Finally he looked around at her. "Wonder if I hadn't ought to get down there and see your lawman, like I started out to?"

Kate Bond felt her face grow hot, and was instantly ashamed of suggesting what she had. It occurred to her then that even her brief acquaintance with this man should have given her the insight to anticipate his doing exactly what he was proposing to do, face out this trouble instead of running from it.

She covered her confusion as well as she could, asking: "You know what you'll run into, don't you?"

Rivers shrugged sparely. "Maybe it won't be as rough as you think. I met Echols in town yesterday. Except for being a bit grouchy, he seemed the right kind."

"They don't come any finer than Jim Echols." She thought of something then that aroused a faint worry in her. "But you can't go back down the way you came, along this trail. Pleasants may be expecting that. He could be waiting for you."

"Then I'll cut off to the south."

She frowned in thought a deliberate moment. Then: "You're welcome to come on home with me. Fred will want to know about this. Fred's my brother. And he'll probably want to go into town to see Jim about this. Why not come with us?"

47

He nodded. "Sounds like sense."

She was much relieved, and also unaccountably pleased at the prospect. "Good," she said. Then, over a slightly awkward pause, she added: "You know half my name. The other half is Bond."

"Kate Bond." Rivers nodded. "I'm Frank Rivers."

She thought she detected a faint nervousness in the way he looked at her, as though he expected some reaction at the mention of his name. But then, as he turned away down the slope toward the mare and the buckskin, he drawled: "Be right with you." His manner was once more unruffled, easy-going.

The gentle rain falling across the valley had turned to snow shortly before dawn this morning. And now at 10:00 the clean whiteness lay fetlock-deep to the horses traveling Ute Springs' streets, contrasting strangely and brilliantly with the gold and orange background of frosted cottonwoods and poplars that hadn't yet shed their leaves.

Jim Echols stared solemnly upon this scene from the window of his small office on the ground floor of the ugly brick courthouse, acutely aware of the three men behind him in the room waiting for his answer to a question Lute Pleasants had just put to him. The Beavertail man's testiness over the past ten minutes had roused in Echols a strong measure of that same annoyance he had felt yesterday during their argument, although he was trying to keep a rein on his temper now in the knowledge that Sam Cauble's violent death gave Pleasants good reason for being out of sorts.

Echols was trying to decide something, whether or not to mention his encounter with Rivers yesterday, whether or not to tell Pleasants that the man was a pardoned convict. And as he debated the wisdom of further infuriating Pleasants, his glance was absent-mindedly following the progress of a buckboard along the snowy street beyond the window.

The rig drew even with the hotel, and abruptly the sheriff's interest quickened as he saw Lola Ames, the hotel owner's daughter, standing on the building's broad verandah. Lola was without a coat and wore a shawl over her shoulders and corn-colored hair. She had evidently been sweeping the porch's edge and now stood, leaning against the railing talking to a woman on the walk below.

Even at this distance her small, narrow-waisted figure was a sight to take a man's eye, and it had its effect on Echols, stirring him as always.

"Well, Echols, how about it?"

The querulous words intruded harshly upon the sheriff's pleasantly straying thoughts, so that, when he swung around and answered, his tone for the first time betrayed his annoyance. "Give a man time to decide."

"Decide what?" Pleasants wanted to know.

"Whether we round up some men, go up there and chouse around in this storm looking for him. Or whether I go down to the depot and have Bert get on the wire. Up above we couldn't spot our man if he was fifty feet away. But we can ask to have the hill trails covered on the far side from Bend and Hilltown. Even as far north as Eagle if you want."

"Why don't we do both?"

Jim Echols shrugged. Though not particularly enthusiastic over the idea, he answered: "Suits me. How many men would you say we need?"

"Twenty, thirty anyway."

The lawman sighed, still convinced that any riding in this weather would be a sheer waste of time. Nevertheless he said—"All right, give me a minute to figure this out."—and half turned toward the window again.

As he glanced back out onto the street, he was once more debating the advantages to be gained from telling Pleasants about Rivers. It halfway angered him that he wanted somehow to protect Rivers until he knew more about this affair. He was positive that if he did tell Pleasants what he knew, the man would take it as proof that Rivers was guilty without question. Equally as important was the fact that, if Pleasants was to learn that Echols had yesterday afternoon mentioned Cauble to Rivers as being lame, then there would be no living with the man.

Pleasants was the kind to nurse a grievance, to magnify it. If he once got it fixed in his mind that Echols had even accidentally been in any way responsible for the killing, he would never forget it. And the lawman had no relish for laying the foundations for such bad feeling.

Suddenly out there on the street Echols was really seeing something he had been staring at sightlessly for the past several seconds. Three riders had passed the hotel intersection and were now turning into the rail adjoining the one where Pleasants and his men had tied their horses. The rider in the lead, dark maroon coat heavily powdered at the shoulders with snow, was Kate Bond. Fred Bond closely followed his sister, riding alongside a tall man on a buckskin, leading a pack animal.

Echols's hawkish face went loose with amazement and disbelief as he recognized that third horseman. He stood a moment in a complete paralysis of surprise. Then, turning abruptly from the window, he stepped to the hallway door, saying unceremoniously: "Stick around, I'll be right back."

The raw air bit sharply into him as he came down the courthouse steps and onto the packed snow of the walk. Coatless and hatless as he was, his appearance caught the immediate attention of Kate and Fred Bond, and of Frank Rivers.

He stopped halfway across the walk, his glance

51

shuttling briefly from Rivers to Fred Bond. "Thanks for bringing him in, Fred."

"Don't thank me. It was his idea."

Bond's words brought the sheriff his second hard surprise of the past half minute. Scarcely able to take in the meaning of what he had heard, he stepped on across to within arm's reach of the buckskin's head and, resting the heel of his right hand on the handle of the gun riding his thigh, said tonelessly: "You've got one hell of a lot of explaining to do."

"Which is why I'm here, Sheriff."

Rivers took in Echols's wary stance and swung down out of the saddle, thinking: *Easy does it. Don't give him a chance to get sore.*

He had no way of knowing that the past ten minutes of talking with Pleasants was in large measure responsible for the lawman's testy manner, so like yesterday during their meeting on the street. All he did know was that Echols seemed chronically ill-tempered and unreasonable, and he found himself almost wishing he had taken his chances on riding over the pass before dawn instead of deciding to come down here.

Because he saw it as being very important that he do everything he could to ease the sheriff's suspicion of him, he now reached in under his coat and unbuckled his shell belt, then stepped across to hand it and the holstered Colt over the rail close to the man.

"Want the rifle, too?" he asked.

"You just stay set. I'll get it."

His move had surprised Echols, whose tone sounded a trifle more conciliatory now. The sheriff took the heavy belt and gun from the rail as Rivers was tying the buckskin, then moved on out to draw the Winchester from its sheath. And Fred Bond, having seen and heard all this, came onto the walk to join Rivers, tilting his head to indicate the three Beavertail horses tied nearby.

"Pleasants in there, Jim?" At Echols's answering nod, he went on: "In that case you've heard only one side of this." He was a slight man a full head shorter than Rivers, and his thin and handsome face showed a strong trace of that same sensitiveness Rivers had noticed earlier in his sister. He was five years older than Kate, twenty-six, and he had known Jim Echols most of his life, so that now his blunt words lost their sting as he added: "You're grown up enough to know what a sorehead Pleasants is. He's given you the wrong slant on this. What're you trying to do with Rivers here, make him a . . . ?"

"He'll have his chance to tell his side of it," the lawman cut in.

Kate Bond came across to stand beside her brother now. She caught Echols's eye as he started back to the walk and her expression was worried, faintly alarmed as she asked: "Why are you arresting him, Jim?"

"Didn't say I was, Kate . . . not yet anyway."

For the first time it seemed to Rivers that the lawman might perhaps be going to listen to reason. And as he followed Kate and her brother into the courthouse hallway, Echols close behind him, he experienced his first faint hope that he hadn't made a bad mistake in returning to Ute Springs.

Following Kate Bond into the office, he first glimpsed the two Beavertail crewmen who had been at his camp with Pleasants this morning. Then as he came through the doorway he found Lute Pleasants standing alongside the room's single window to his right.

The Beavertail owner's stony glance settled on him and didn't stray. "Did you serve that warrant, Sheriff?"

"Not yet." The lawman closed the door, stepped around Rivers and over to his desk, laying the rifle and the holstered .44 on it. "But maybe I will before we're through."

"Maybe? What's to stop you from doing it now?"

"We'll listen to what he has to say first." The sheriff glanced at Pleasants's two men. "Room's crowded, boys. You two wait outside."

"They stay where they are," Pleasants at once insisted.

This past quarter hour had left Jim Echols with his nerves slightly frayed. And now his irritation once again got the best of him. "This is the sheriff's office, Pleasants. I'm the sheriff, remember? I say they get out."

The sultry anger showing in Pleasants's dark eyes brightened momentarily as he returned Echols's bridling stare. But then he gave a grudging nod, whereupon Harry and Ben stepped around Kate, who had taken off her coat and was standing with her back to the stove. Neither man so much as glanced at Rivers as they came past him and went out into the hallway.

Fred Bond had no sooner closed the door after them than Jim Echols eased down into his chair behind the desk, picked up Rivers's Winchester, and began levering the shells from its magazine. Pleasants watched him empty it, leave the action open, and hold it to the window's light as he looked down the barrel.

"Clean. Some dust there at the muzzle," the lawman finally remarked, offering Pleasants the weapon.

Pleasants examined the rifle only cursorily, afterward saying—"Look over his other iron."— as he laid the Winchester on the desk.

A weighty silence lay across the room as Echols punched the shells from the Colt, removed its pin, and rolled out the cylinder. After holding it to the light, he handed it across to the Beavertail man, dryly commenting: "More dust."

Once again Pleasants spent little time in his examination. Handing the .44 back to Echols, he said flatly: "Now let's hear this trumped-up story."

The sheriff glanced obliquely up at Rivers. "Go ahead, tell it, Rivers."

"Rivers?"

Pleasants's involuntary exclamation was soft-spoken. His expression took on a fleeting, hard alertness. But then he quickly recovered from his astonishment and added with the same truculence as before: "So that's what they call you. Well, let's hear what you've got to say. And make it the truth."

Frank Rivers had been trying to puzzle out what lay behind Jim Echols's stern but fair approach to this matter. The lawman was being more reason-able now than he had been five minutes ago on the street, and far more reasonable than he had been yesterday.

Unable to fathom this change in the sheriff, his attention had a moment ago strayed to Kate Bond, so that he didn't witness the brief change in Pleasants's manner. The man's words meant nothing to him beyond the fact of Pleasants's being only mildly curious on hearing his name.

This was the first time he had seen Kate Bond when she wasn't wearing the bulky wool coat. Back at Anchor she had changed from her work clothes and was now wearing a blue print shirtwaist and a black wool riding skirt, divided so that she had ridden man-fashion on the way down to town.

She was, he saw, a tall and slender girl with a natural grace and poise. Her upper body was gently rounded and the narrow-waisted, bulky skirt failed to hide the slim line of her hips. The light from the lamp on the sheriff's desk laid reddish highlights across her hair. And her eyes just now, intercepting his look, smiled at him as though she wanted to put him at ease and lend encouragement.

He put aside his strong awareness of her, looking across at Echols to say: "What I have isn't much. This man Cauble rode in on my camp sometime after three this morning. I was building up the fire and he caught me flat-footed. He held a rifle on me while he combed me over for cutting his fence. He said . . ."

"Which you damn' well did cut!" Pleasants brusquely interjected.

"Let's let him finish." Jim Echols's tone was strangely unruffled. "Go ahead, Rivers. What happened then?"

"Cauble claimed I was working for Anchor, which was the first time I'd ever heard of the outfit. He was working himself up to taking me back down with him when this shot came from up the trail."

"What proof's he got of all that, Echols?"

"This much, Lute," Kate Bond quietly inserted. "Old Wade heard the shot, got to worrying about it, and came up to the house to waken Fred. That was at three-thirty, exactly."

"Go on, Rivers," Echols said matter-of-factly.

"That's about it." Rivers thought back, shortly adding: "Except that when it got light, I loaded him onto his jughead and was all set to bring him back down here when company arrived."

"How do we know he wasn't set to pack Sam up into the hills and bury him?" Pleasants wanted to know.

His barbed question fanned alive a flare of anger in Rivers. And before the sheriff could speak, Rivers drawled: "If I'd cut your friend down, why would I hang around? Between when he was shot and the time you hit my camp, I could've been over the pass with my tracks snowed over and your man planted so deep no one would ever find him, as you say."

For some seconds a tense silence lay across the room, the only sound being the gentle sighing of the stove. Echols was blandly eyeing Pleasants, waiting for some comment and, oddly enough, faintly smiling.

At length Pleasants's jaw tightened and he stated tonelessly: "Sam Cauble's dead, Sheriff. My fence is cut. Add the two together and what answer do you come up with?"

"You tell me."

"Just one. Anchor hired this hardcase to cut fence. Sam had the bad luck to stumble across him last . . ."

"That's a damned lie."

Fred Bond, who had so far kept his strict silence, spoke softly but in deadly seriousness. Hearing what he had from this ordinarily mild-spoken man, Jim Echols instantly straightened in his chair to say: "Here now. Cool off, both of you." He came up out of his chair then. "I know how you feel, Pleasants. But look at the facts. There's no sign of Rivers having used these irons lately. Cauble's hadn't been fired, either. Rivers didn't run when he could have. More than that, he came down here on his own hook. He . . ."

"What was he doing up there above my fence last night?"

"Now maybe I can just answer that," Echols replied. "It so happens I ran into him here in town yesterday afternoon and had a few words with him. At the time he mentioned going over the hills by way of the old trail. He was just on his way through."

For the first time now Pleasants seemed unsure of himself. "Why didn't you tell me all this before?"

"Why should I?" the lawman countered. "But think this over. If Anchor had hired him to cut fence, then he'd have kept clear of me, wouldn't he?"

He waited for Pleasants to argue this and, when the man didn't, stated with a definite finality: "He's to be at the inquest this afternoon and let a jury listen to his story. If nothing new turns up, then as far as I'm concerned he's free as the breeze."

Lute Pleasants didn't like this and there was fire in his dark eyes now. "If he didn't kill Sam, who did?"

"Wish I knew, Pleasants. One day I will, and that's a promise."

The Beavertail man glanced at Rivers. "Did you see anyone else at all up there?"

"Only your man."

Pleasants's bafflement and stubborn indignation were very convincing as he eyed the sheriff and nodded to indicate Rivers. "I told you how he braced us up there, dared us to take him. You've got your killer right here in front of you."

"There you go, running off at the mouth again." Rivers's flat drawl came hard on the heels of the other's testy words. "Someday it'll get you into real trouble. Like it almost did up there this morning."

He waited for Pleasants to say something. When nothing came, he glanced at Echols. "They had a man behind me. I had the luck to spot him before he could do what he was told, draw a bead on my back. What should I have done, let them take me and either string me up right there or beat my brains out?"

"Let's stop clawin' at each other," Echols inserted impatiently, as though he wanted to get this over with as soon as possible. "We'll see what the inquest turns up."

"Which'll be nothing at all." Having registered

his complete disgust, Lute Pleasants abruptly stalked across the room and went out the door, slamming it hard behind him.

"Sweet-tempered cuss," Fred Bond dryly observed.

It seemed that Jim Echols hadn't heard. He sat now with elbows on the arms of his tilted-back chair, chin resting on his clasped hands as he narrowly regarded Rivers. And with the silence weighing more heavily with each passing second, both Kate and Fred sensed the change in his manner and stared at him in growing puzzlement.

Suddenly the lawman hit the desk top a booming blow with fisted right hand. "Now, by God," he exploded, "we'll have the truth!"

When Rivers said nothing, the lawman's glance strayed briefly, angrily to Fred and the girl. "Know who we got here?" he asked tonelessly. "Did friend Rivers tell you he's just finished getting four years of free board and lodging from the territory?"

Kate's stunned and bewildered glance swung quickly to Rivers. And Fred Bond breathed sharply—"What's this?"—as his surprised stare followed his sister's.

"Go ahead, Sheriff. Get out your knife and hack away," Rivers said quietly. "But why didn't you start it sooner, while Pleasants was here?"

"Because I damn' well want to keep him off my back, not yours."

Echols's look had been smug, yet now it

changed subtly, his thin face reddened in anger. "Kate, Fred, the governor handed this man a pardon a while back."

The girl was eyeing Rivers in a mutely appealing way so eloquent of her wanting to believe in him that he was almost, but not quite, tempted to speak for himself. Instead, he said: "Echols doesn't believe in pardons."

"Not in this one, I don't. Tell them how you got it. Tell 'em why you were put behind the bars in the first place."

"You know the story, you tell it."

"Don't think I won't." The lawman's now-furious scowl shuttled to Kate and her brother. "This man was tried and sentenced for life for killing his father. For filling his father's back full of buckshot in a stage hold-up with another man near Peak City, up north five years ago. How do I know? Because my cousin was driver of the stage. They beat Bill, left him for dead. But he lived. He's a cripple now, livin' . . ."

"That's not true, is it?"

Softly as she had spoken, Kate's hushed and horrified exclamation halted Echols in mid-sentence. The girl's face had lost its color and her greenish hazel eyes showed outrage and disbelief. She was strikingly beautiful now as she eyed Rivers, insisting: "It isn't, is it?"

"Not a word of it."

The sheriff snorted scornfully. "Twelve men

on a jury thought so, Kate. Bill heard this . . ."

"Just a minute, Jim." The girl's glance hadn't strayed from Rivers as she cut Echols short the second time. "I want to hear this from the man who knows exactly what happened."

Frank Rivers sighed deeply in frustration, for the moment feeling beyond his depth in trying to say anything in the face of the lawman's barbed antagonism. Nonetheless he stubbornly began: "The night of the killing I was a three-day ride north of Peak City, headed for my homestead up in the Bighorns. That night I camped along a road with a drummer, an old man peddling a wagon-load of odds and ends from town to town. The next day, when I turned up at the homestead, they had a deputy waiting to arrest me."

"Then why would they think you had anything to do with it?"

It was Fred Bond who put the question. And before Rivers had a chance to answer, Echols was speaking for him. "Why? Because Bill, this cousin of mine, heard Rivers's partner call him by name that night. Not once but twice. The first time it was 'Rivers,' the next time 'Frank.' Bill swore to that in court."

The sheriff looked up at Rivers derisively now. "How much did the two of you get out of that Wells, Fargo strongbox? Twelve thousand in dust, wasn't it?"

When Rivers only shook his head helplessly in

63

answer, Kate asked hollowly: "Is all this true, Frank?"

Hearing her call him by his given name subtly conveyed to Rivers the fact that this girl, for some inexplicable reason, was still wanting to believe in him. And there was a deep humility in him as he told her: "Yes. That's the story that came out at the trial."

"You got a different one?" Fred Bond wanted to know.

Rivers nodded, leaning back against the wall. "Yes. Echols will tell you that my father and I were on the outs, that . . ."

"On the outs, you call it?" The lawman laughed dryly. "Fred, him and his old man had come close to a knock down and drag out only three days before this happened. In front of witnesses."

Once again Rivers nodded. "That's true. As far as it goes." He was speaking to Kate now. "My father ran the Wells, Fargo office in Peak City. There was, and still is, a lot of easy money to be picked up working around the diggings. He thought that's what I should be doing, salting the dollars away. I didn't. I'd built up this Bighorn homestead and wanted to raise cattle. That's what our scrap was about."

Fred Bond said: "Jim, this doesn't prove a thing. Kate can tell you that the old man and I never saw exactly eye to eye, the good Lord rest his soul."

64

"It helped prove something at Rivers's trial, though," Echols testily stated.

"It did," Rivers admitted. "But only because I couldn't produce my one witness, this peddler I'd camped with the night the stage was held up. Which," he added dryly, "brings up the question of my pardon our friend here doesn't like."

"Who the hell does like it?" The sheriff gave Kate a brief, apologetic glance. "I'm one of maybe half a thousand people that think you bought your way out of prison with the gold you got off the stage that night."

Trying to ignore those acid words, a rough edge creeping into his tone, Rivers said: "It took my lawyer better than four years to locate that old drummer and bring him back to see the judge who sat at my trial. Once the judge heard his story, he went to see the governor. There was a court hearing and they turned me loose."

Jim Echols snorted in disgust. "They'll be arguin' that pardon up in Peak City for the . . ."

"What kind of a hard-headed joker are you, Echols?" Rivers cut in sharply, unable any longer to hold his temper in check. "I spent four years in a stinking hole of a prison because the law made a mistake. Now you sit there making another. What does a man have to do to live down something he never did?"

The sheriff's face turned livid. He came slowly up out of his chair and leaned forward, hands gripping the edge of his desk. "Listen, you. I was raised with Bill Echols, the same as if he'd been my brother. He's crippled now, he'll never walk again. Someone half beat the life out of him. If it wasn't you, who was it?"

"That's what I'm trying to find out. That's why I came here. You know that."

Echols suddenly made a chopping gesture with one hand. "The hell with this." He was furious, trembling as he reached to his pocket and brought out a bunch of keys. Jerking a thumb toward a heavy door set midway the length of the office's back wall, he said brittlely: "In you go. You're going to stay locked up till time for the inquest. And my hunch is you'll . . ."

"Jim, none of this is fair," Kate said in a low voice.

"Fair, Kate? Was he playin' fair when he beat in the back of Bill's skull, then caved in his side kickin' him after he'd fallen into the road off the stage that night?"

Doggedly the lawman stepped over and pulled open the door of the jail. Nodding curtly, he motioned Rivers to join him. And as the tall man stepped past Kate and came toward him, he backed away and drew the gun from the holster riding his thigh, holding it lined at Rivers.

As the two disappeared into the jail, Kate asked in a hushed voice: "What's come over him, Fred? It isn't like him to kick a man when he's down."

Fred Bond sighed, answering as unconcernedly as he could: "We'll have a talk with him when he comes back out."

They waited, hearing the rattle of a cell door being unlocked in the jail, hearing the door clang shut, and the key being turned again in the lock. Then Jim Echols reappeared and pushed the heavy oak door of the jail shut, locking it with a big key.

"Jim, let's cool down and think this over," Fred said as the sheriff turned from the door. "Here's a man who was ready to bring a body down here of his own accord, his irons clean, and . . ."

"That's got nothing to do with this other," the lawman cut in sharply.

"But it does, Jim," Kate insisted. "You're not trying this man over again. He's been pardoned for that other. All you're interested in is whether or not he killed Cauble. And you don't have a bit of proof that he did."

The sheriff tossed his keys onto the desk so viciously that they slid off and dropped to the floor. He wheeled on Kate abruptly, asking: "What am I to do? Just turn him loose?"

"He turned himself over to you, Jim. You looked at his guns." Kate smiled then, her eyes pleading with him for understanding. "If you tell about his past at the inquest, he hasn't a chance."

"I don't want him to have a chance. Not one."

"But suppose you're wrong? Suppose he's inno-cent? Suppose he's tried here for killing Cauble?

And suppose they hang him? How would you feel if it came out later you'd been mistaken?"

The intensity of her words finally penetrated the hard shell of Jim Echols's unreason. He shook his head now, sighing mightily as he grumbled: "Don't ask a man questions he can't answer."

"She's right. You've got to answer them before it's too late." Fred Bond put his back to the stove close alongside his sister, shortly continuing: "Sure, you've got your ideas on his pardon. But what was that he said . . . something about his reason for being here?"

"His reason for bein' here," the sheriff echoed derisively. "Know what he's doin'? He's ridin' the country lettin' on like he's lookin' for a lame carpenter."

"What's a lame carpenter got to do with this?" Fred asked.

"The night the stage was held up, Bill got a good look at one of the pair that did it. He swears this man was lame. Well, it seems there'd been a lame carpenter putting a new roof on the Wells, Fargo shack in Peak City the week before this all happened. But he turned up drunk on the job three mornings straight runnin', so Rivers's old man fired him. They tried to locate him for the trial as a witness, because he'd listened in on this scrap Rivers had with his father. But by then they couldn't locate him." Smiling in a belittling way, Echols went on: "Rivers claims this carpenter could have known when the gold was being shipped. And the carpenter, knowin' about the fight he'd had with his father, used his name that night to frame the killin' on him. If I remember rightly, Rivers even claims they meant Bill to live so he could say he'd heard the name used."

For a long moment after the lawman finished speaking, no one said anything. It was Kate who finally asked: "Couldn't Frank be right about all this?"

"I don't believe so for a minute. It's too far-fetched."

Kate glanced at Fred now before putting another question. "And you're going to tell all this at the inquest, Jim?"

"Don't know yet, Kate. It's a tricky thing to decide."

"You know what this'll mean to Lute Pleasants, don't you?" she pointedly asked. "He'll hit the roof because you didn't tell him sooner. And if I know Lute, he'll see that Rivers stands trial for killing Sam Cauble." She was eyeing the lawman coldly now as she added: "That would be something for you to be proud of, wouldn't it, Jim?"

The withering scorn in her tone made Jim Echols protest: "Lord, Kate, you act like I . . . like . . ."

When he didn't finish, Kate took her coat from the back of the chair sitting against the wall nearby. "Well, Fred, I guess we've done all we can," she said. "Let's get out of here."

She was on her way to the door, coat thrown over arm, before Echols managed to blurt out: "Now listen, Kate. You've got to look at my side of this."

If the girl heard him, she gave no sign of it as she opened the door and stepped out into the hallway. And Fred, following her, paused at the door to glance around at the lawman and slowly shake his head, nothing else, before he pulled the door shut.

CHAPTER FIVE

Lute Pleasants could still feel the numbness, the shock that had gripped him on hearing Jim Echols first call the tall stranger by name. Rivers! He had been jolted hard in the beginning, and almost as hard as each repetition of the name drove home the conviction that this just might be Frank Rivers, son of the man he had shot that night with Sam Cauble on the stage road below Peak City.

Here was the one name on the face of the earth Pleasants had any reason whatsoever to fear now that Sam Cauble was dead. And for the first few minutes after leaving the courthouse—having told Ben and Harry to meet him after the inquest—he had come close to being panicked as he wondered what Frank Rivers's presence in Ute Springs could mean.

If his first name is Frank, he kept telling himself. *If* . . .

He was standing in a store entrance two doors below the hotel when Kate and Fred Bond left the courthouse and rode their horses down to the livery, leading Rivers's buckskin and mare. The fact of their taking the two animals with them was sobering; it probably meant that Echols was holding Rivers under arrest.

71

This was something Pleasants had wanted to see happen an hour ago. Now it was the last thing he wanted, for if this should turn out to be the Peak City Frank Rivers it was all-important to him to see the man quickly on his way out of the country. *If he's the one,* he told himself once more.

Last summer he had read a caustic newspaper editorial criticizing Frank Rivers's pardon and belittling Rivers's statement that he was going to try and clear his name by finding further proof of what had really happened the night his father died. And the more Pleasants thought about it now, the more it seemed that, if this was Frank Rivers, he might be hunting for some trace of the two men who had stopped the stage that night.

This had no sooner occurred to him than he was starkly remembering that Sam Cauble had been talking to Rivers just before the bullet had knocked him out of the saddle this morning. For one dread, nerve-wearing minute, Pleasants's face felt clammy and cold as he wondered whether Sam had recognized Rivers. If so, it was very possible that Sam had been galled enough, or drunk enough, to let Rivers know that the man who had shot his father was right here almost within his reach. That could well be the reason Rivers had come back to town instead of heading over the pass this morning.

Pleasants had little time to dwell on this frightening possibility, for just then he saw Echols come out of the courthouse and head this way across the street. Guessing that the sheriff was on his way to the hotel for his noon meal, Pleasants started up the walk. And Jim Echols, seeing him approaching, stopped and waited for him at the foot of the hotel verandah steps.

"Well, your man's locked up," the lawman bluntly announced as Pleasants joined him.

Pleasants had already guessed this but nonetheless asked: "Why?"

"Why?" The lawman's look was one of unfeigned amazement. "God Almighty, didn't you swear out a warrant on him?"

"I mean . . . why, when you were all set to turn him loose?"

"A warrant's a warrant. You said to arrest him, so I did."

Lute Pleasants had no way of knowing just then that Echols's tart rejoinder was tempered by his disagreement with Fred and Kate Bond.

"Now hold on, Sheriff." The Beavertail man spoke mildly, placatingly. "I only meant to lock him up if you were sure he really . . . by the way, what did you call him?"

"Rivers. Frank Rivers."

Once again Pleasants felt that now-familiar numbness knife through him, though he gave no outward indication of it, his tone calm and unruffled as he asked: "Did you get more out of him than I heard?"

Echols hesitated slightly before answering: "Not a thing."

"You don't think he put the bullet through Sam?"

"I don't. But it's not for me to say. Let the coroner decide."

Pleasants shook his head as though completely baffled. "I've been thinkin' about this. It's serious business. Maybe I was too steamed up a while ago to see it straight. But so would you have been if you'd come across him the way I did, Sam loaded across his hull like a sack of feed."

"No one says you don't have a right to be good and sore."

Pleasants frowned now, saying seriously: "Y'know, I'm beginning to think Rivers couldn't have killed Sam."

Jim Echols's jaw came partly open in surprise. "You can say that after all the hell you raised?"

"After all the hell I raised." The Beavertail man managed a guilty smile. "Sorry, Sheriff, but a man doesn't see his foreman killed every day. It took me some time to see things straight."

The lawman was hopelessly confused now. Some minutes ago his dignity had suffered considerably at the hands of two of his close friends, Kate and Fred. Now his arbitrary stand of not giving Frank Rivers the benefit of any doubt whatsoever was being cut from under him by Pleasants's change of mind.

So there was real venom in his words as he drawled: "Then I'm to turn him loose? Just like that?"

"Guess so, Sheriff," Pleasants blandly replied. "At least, don't hold him on my warrant."

Jim Echols's eyes went narrow-lidded in righteous anger. "Has it struck you that none of this would've happened if it hadn't been for your damned fence?"

"We'll leave the fence out of this."

Giving the man a parting look bridling with scorn, Jim Echols turned away and stalked back across the street fully realizing what a ridiculous position Pleasants's change of mind had placed him in. As he felt the feathery touch of swirling snowflakes against his face, he was starkly confronted with having to make the choice Kate had so clearly pointed out to him some minutes ago.

With little or no evidence against Rivers—in fact, with evidence in the man's favor—he could nevertheless probably see the man jailed and tried for this murder by simply relating the details of the Peak City killing. His instinct was to want to do just this so as to square things for Bill Echols. But as he approached the courthouse entrance, he was for the first time listening to the voice of a small doubt. It was just possible, remotely so, that Kate and Fred had been right in suggesting that Rivers could be innocent of any involvement in the Peak City affair. If this latter turned out to be the case, then Echols knew there would be no living with his conscience.

The hell with the whole mess! was his angry thought as he pulled open the courthouse door.

The stale warmth of the hallway was welcome after the biting cold outside. And Echols was thinking back to his reason for having gone across to the hotel just now—the prospect of seeing Lola Ames and perhaps of eating the noon meal with her—as he reached to his pocket for the keys, sorted out the office door key, and thrust it into the lock.

The key wouldn't turn. The door was unlocked. He twisted the knob and opened the door, thinking that he had been very careless in leaving the office open.

He stepped on into the room, then suddenly jerked to a halt. For now he remembered clearly having locked this door less than five minutes ago.

A strong alarm was running through him even as he glanced across the room. The heavy jail door stood wide open.

CHAPTER SIX

There was little need for Jim Echols to cross the office and peer into his jail to know that Frank Rivers was gone. Yet he did just that, seeing the grating to the outside cell in which he had locked Rivers swung far back on its hinges. The man had somehow managed to unlock all three doors, the one to the cell, the one to the jail, the one leading to the hallway.

By now, Echols supposed, Rivers had probably left the livery, where he might have guessed he would find his buckskin once he saw that his animals were no longer tied in front of the courthouse. It all at once struck the lawman that there was now a very strong likelihood of Rivers having killed Sam Cauble. As he wheeled and hurried across his office, his long shelving jaw was set tightly in grim satisfaction. He had been right about Rivers after all.

He supposed Rivers could have no more than a ten-minute lead on him, if that much. In ten more minutes he could have twenty men, thirty, in the saddle and riding out to cover the roads and trails. Rivers, a stranger to the country, had not the slightest chance of outriding men who knew the range around Ute Springs as well as they knew their own back yards.

77

"Sheriff!"

The word was spoken sharply from behind Echols. He halted in mid-stride, hand outstretched to open the hallway door. He swung quickly around.

The jail door had swung partway shut. Rivers was stepping from behind it. He swung it back against the wall once more, his flat-planed face wearing a serious look that didn't change in the slightest as the lawman quickly brushed his coat aside and lifted his gun from its holster.

Only when the Colt muzzle was lined squarely at him did Rivers glance down at his empty waist and then across at the desk.

"Why that?" he asked. "There mine are. Right where you left them."

The sheriff had drawn instinctively, without thought. His glance shuttled briefly to the desk now to see Rivers's .44 and Winchester, and the shells from both weapons, lying as they had been for the past hour. He had forgotten all about Rivers's guns, hadn't noticed them.

Slowly then, still surprised but also very suspicious, Jim Echols let his .45 fall to his side, then holstered it. "What the devil you trying to pull here, Rivers?"

"I wanted to see if I could pound something into your hard head, Sheriff."

"Like what?" The lawman's face took on color.

"Like letting you know I could have given you the slip. Instead, here I am. Because," Rivers added brittlely, "I damned well didn't put that bullet through Cauble."

Confused as he was, Echols did manage to grasp the fact that there was a certain amount of unarguable logic behind the words. He halfway understood that the man could scarcely have produced stronger evidence than this of his good intentions. Rivers had broken out of jail, had had the chance to make a getaway. Yet here he was, as he had pointed out.

All the sheriff could think of to say just now was: "How did you do it?"

"Open the locks?" With an unamused smile, Frank Rivers ran a thumb inside his belt and brought out a six-inch blade of spring steel with a series of unequal-length slots cut in one end. Holding it in the palm of his right hand, he said tonelessly: "That four years of free board and lodging you mentioned taught me a thing or two. Part of the time they had me locked up with a man who could pick the best lock ever made."

Thrusting the blade inside his belt again, he nodded toward the desk. "So I could've waited there by the door and caught you, couldn't I? Knocked you cold, stuffed your mouth, and locked you into your own jail. By the time you'd have been missed at the inquest, I could have been long gone, Sheriff. In this storm you wouldn't have had a prayer of catching up with me. Now just ask yourself why I didn't do all this."

Jim Echols suddenly knew without any doubt whatsoever that an innocent man stood before him, a man innocent of having put the bullet into Sam Cauble. As to the Peak City affair, he still had his rock-solid conviction, for his mind had been too long cemented with the certainty that Rivers's pardon had been a miscarriage of justice.

It was typical of him that, once proven wrong, he took the most direct means of making amends. Without so much as a word now, he stepped across to his desk, picked up Rivers's .44, opened its loading gate, and dropped the five shells into its cylinder, afterward thrusting it in its holster and offering the heavy shell belt to Rivers. And as Rivers came across and took the weapon, Echols filled the Winchester's magazine.

Handing the rifle across, he said matter-of-factly: "Fred took your jugheads down to the livery. You're to be at Doc Lightfoot's house for the inquest at one o'clock. Anyone can tell you where Doc lives."

Rivers belted on the handgun, tied the holster thong about his thigh. For a long moment he stood waiting, as though expecting the sheriff to say something further. Finally he asked: "That's all?"

"That's all."

"What'll Pleasants say to this? Suppose I run into him?"

"Just had a talk with him. He's been thinking it over and said to tear up the warrant."

Frank Rivers's thick brows lifted in surprise. "So?" he drawled. Then, getting no response from Echols, the rifle in hand, he crossed to the hallway door.

He had opened it and was about to step from the room when he thought of something that made him pause and turn to say: "One day I'll know the truth about what happened up there below Peak City that night, Sheriff. When I do, I'll let you know."

"Do that."

The lawman's words were dry as alkali dust, unfriendly. And with a faint wondering shrug Frank Rivers turned out into the hallway, pulling the door shut behind him.

CHAPTER SEVEN

Kate Bond, coming out onto the porch of Doc Lightfoot's house as the medico's parlor emptied, was feeling a trifle bewildered but very happy. The inquest was over, having lasted a scant half hour. Sam Cauble had, according to the jury's verdict, "met his death at the hands of a person or persons unknown."

It was still hard for Kate to believe that Lute Pleasants hadn't questioned so much as one point of Frank Rivers's story to the coroner. Nor had Jim Echols even hinted that he doubted what the man had had to say. The sheriff had simply stated the facts as he knew them, had given the opinion that Rivers's guns couldn't have been fired recently. Best of all, there had been no mention of Rivers's past or pardon.

For the past two hours Kate had been deeply concerned over the outcome of the inquest. And now, seeing Jim Echols come onto the porch following two other men, she stepped over to take him by the arm and lead him aside from the group standing near the door.

"Jim, I could hug you for giving Frank his chance." The warmth in her eyes was eloquent of her relief as she added uncertainly: "I thought you were going to . . . But that doesn't matter now. Thanks for what you did."

Echols didn't respond as she had expected he might. His expression was stern, almost unfriendly as he told her: "At least we'll be rid of him."

She was jolted hard by his acid manner and responded in a hushed voice: "This isn't like you, Jim. Give the man a . . ."

"Look, Kate. I won't be sold a bill of goods. By you or anyone else. So let's forget this joker and hope we've seen the last of him."

He turned abruptly away from her then as Doc Lightfoot called to him from the doorway, and went back into the house. And Kate, sobered by what he had said and by his bull-headedness, looked out onto the street that was lightly hazed by the lazily falling snow, trying to understand why he could be so unforgiving and intolerant toward Rivers when he was ordinarily a man who went out of his way to be fair and just in all things.

She had little time to reflect upon the enigma, for right then a voice said behind her: "Kate, help me persuade this stubborn cuss."

She turned and found Fred and Rivers standing close behind her, Rivers with rifle cradled across his arm.

"I've offered him a job with us and he won't take it," Fred went on. Good-naturedly he added: "Guess he has us pegged as a bad luck outfit."

"You're wrong there," Rivers was quick to say.

Meeting his glance, Kate felt a stir of strangely pleasurable excitement over the possibility Fred had raised. "We could keep you busy, Frank. Has Fred told you . . . ?"

"I've told him everything, Sis. About the fence, about having to . . ."

Fred checked his words, a frown settling across his face as he watched Lute Pleasants cross the porch and go down the steps and out the walk. He gave Kate a questioning look. "Wonder what came over friend Lute?"

When she only shook her head, he glanced at Rivers. "I'd have laid money he was ready to rip you wide open."

"So would I." Rivers shrugged, adding: "Anyway, he's my main reason for not taking you up upon your offer."

"Pleasants? Why?"

"My being around might give him just one more excuse to make trouble for you." Over a moment's awkward hesitation in which he soberly eyed Kate, Rivers went on: "Let's put it this way. If you're really up against it, I'll stay, and gladly. But if you can hire another man in place of me, I ought to be drifting. There's a lot of settlements over in the Haystacks I can give a look-see before winter shuts in."

"Looking for your lame carpenter?" Kate asked.

At Rivers's answering nod, she felt a stab of

keen disappointment, nonetheless telling Fred: "He's right. We can find another man."

Fred was reluctantly tilting his head in agreement as Rivers wanted to know: "Why can't you make a deal with this man Crowe you mention? Bring your beef out across his range? You say you're bound to take losses driving over the pass to Bend. So why not try and figure what they'd be and offer Crowe say a quarter of that figure? Either in money or animals."

"That's a sound thought," Fred conceded. "But Crowe's the kind that'd say no out of plain spite. Years ago our father had him arrested for rustling. They let him off, but he's never wasted much love on Anchor since."

"You should ride across to Summit and see him, Fred."

"Guess I will, Sis. Tomorrow maybe." Nodding toward the street, Fred asked: "Ready to go?"

They left the porch and walked toward where they had left their animals, Rivers feeling ill at ease and a little ashamed of his decision. And as they went through the gate and toward the tie rail, he said sheepishly: "This is a poor way of paying you back for all you've done for me."

"Of paying us back? It's only because of Anchor that you got into this mess," was Fred's rejoinder.

"Forget that part of it," Rivers said.

He went on out to the buckskin then, thrust the Winchester in its scabbard, and wiped the fluffy snow from his saddle. He had his back to the house, had lifted boot to stirrup, and was swinging up into leather when a rough-edged voice spoke from behind him: "Rivers!"

Settling into the saddle, he looked across to see Jim Echols standing on the walk. The sheriff's clipped word had taken Kate's and Fred's attention. And now as the lawman spoke once again, they were eyeing him closely, listening.

"What I said yesterday still goes," the lawman intoned flatly. "When you hit the county line, keep goin'."

Rivers only nodded sparely. But Fred Bond stiffened in the saddle, saying hotly: "Jim, get that burr out the seat of your pants. How much does a man have to take from you?"

Echols paid Fred not the slightest notice as he said: "You'll do well to take the long way around today. That pass'll be drifted tight shut."

"So I'd intended."

"Then haul your freight. And don't come back!"

Rivers glanced around at Fred and Kate, lifting a hand to touch his hat, saying—"So long."—as he reined the buckskin out onto the street, winding the pack mare's lead rope about the horn of his saddle.

CHAPTER EIGHT

About to leave Doc Lightfoot's house after the inquest, Lute Pleasants had come to the door to find Fred Bond and Rivers talking to Kate directly beyond on the porch. In his furtive way, he had paused just short of the open doorway and had plainly overheard Fred tell his sister of having offered Rivers a job at Anchor.

For perhaps half a minute a hard apprehension had held Pleasants motionless. By the time he finally came onto the porch, he had gathered enough from their conversation to make him fairly certain that Rivers wasn't taking the job. But then as he walked on up the street toward the center of town, common sense told him that Rivers might change his mind.

He decided he must know what choice Rivers had made. If the man stayed in this country, he represented a real and constant danger. If he left, he could be forgotten.

Harry and Ben were waiting for him in the Bon Ton. He motioned them away from the bar and led the way back onto the street.

"You two better make tracks for camp," he told them. "Ben, you're in charge from now on. Tomorrow mend the cuts in the wire and then get on with putting in the posts at the far end."

Ben Galt nodded. "Anything else?"

"Yes. On your way up, swing across to the layout. Put a wagon box on that set of runners behind the barn, then load that big scoop and haul it as far as where the creek cuts through the fence. Run the sled into the willows down below the fence so it's out of sight." As an afterthought, Pleasants added: "Oh, another thing. You'll find a couple pair of gum boots in the wagon shed. Bring them along."

Harry, who had a lively curiosity, asked: "We diggin' ditches this time of year?"

"Tell you later," was Pleasants's evasive answer. "By the way, forget the night hawking unless we run into more trouble. Now get along so you'll be back in camp in time for supper."

"Another of Red's meals is sure goin' to be a treat," Galt sourly observed as they walked away.

So it was, some ten minutes later, that Pleasants saw Frank Rivers ride up the street leading the pack mare. He went immediately to the livery, got his horse, and left town in the opposite direction, to all appearances on his way back to Beavertail. Yet, once beyond sight of the last house along the street, he climbed the creek bluff and made a long, fast circle to the east and then into the south that in half an hour brought him within sight of the pass road some four miles above town.

Standing his horse in a clump of balsam above the road, he presently saw Rivers ride past. As the man disappeared into the fog of snow settling steadily out of the sooty sky, Pleasants felt a lessening of the worry that had been plaguing him. It looked as though Rivers was on his way out of the country.

Twice more, by circling, the Beavertail owner glimpsed his quarry steadily climbing the pass road. And with the early evening sky clearing before a stiff, bitter-cold wind whistling down off the peaks, he was looking down on dusk-shadowed Summit from the shelter of the spruce forest above the shabby settlement to see Rivers ride through it as far as the log barn and corral of Bannister's stage station.

He watched Rivers disappear into the barn, and once when the whine of the wind died away, he faintly heard a voice calling from the cabin on the knoll above the big corral. Directly afterward he watched Rivers climb the path to the cabin carrying bedroll and rifle.

Pleasants was disappointed. He had expected to see Rivers over the pass before dark, riding out of sight and out of mind. Yet he could still be fairly certain that the man would do exactly that in the morning. And with this satisfying thought he had turned back and started down the cañon, coat collar shielding his face from the wind-driven snow, when suddenly something occurred to him that made him draw rein.

He had had it in mind for several days now to

see Phil Crowe about stringing fence beyond the line of the Beavertail so as to deny Anchor access to the low country from this south side of its range, that touchy subject having been one of the reasons for his quarrel with Sam Cauble yesterday afternoon. Crowe's saloon, the Pat Hand, lay right below here on Summit's crooked street. Now, Pleasants decided, would be as good a time as any to see Crowe. And in the thickening dusk he turned down toward the town.

CHAPTER NINE

T he settlement of Summit didn't much impress a man. Riding its crooked street, Rivers saw the grimy windows of only two buildings showing lamplight against the gathering dusk. Most of the shacks and shanties and cabins appeared deserted, some with boarded-up windows, others with their steep-pitched roofs caved in, collapsed by the weight of the heavy snows of past winters.

The place had a look of disuse about it that nonetheless made a man wonder if he wasn't being watched, that made him suspect that there would be furtive comings and goings once darkness settled in. For this near-deserted town set deep in its timbered notch appeared to be the kind of place that invariably attracted the night riders, the ones on the high lonesome. It had a secretive, faintly sinister air about it.

At the upper end of town Rivers came abreast a corral and a hump-roofed barn in good repair. Over the barn's wide door a sign proclaimed:

Inter-Mountain Stages, Rooms. Meals.
S.L. Bannister, Prop.

It had been Rivers's plan to cross the pass this evening and camp somewhere on the far side. But now, because he had been worrying something around in his mind on the way up here, and because the thought of a home-cooked meal suddenly made him realize he was very hungry, he gave the sign his prolonged attention, reining in on the buckskin and afterward noticing a white-chinked log cabin sitting on a knoll a hundred yards removed from the road.

He thought: *The food's probably not worth throwing out.* Yet there was a restlessness in him, a dissatisfaction over the way he had so summarily turned down Fred Bond's offer this afternoon. And it was this alone that shortly prompted him to swing the buckskin over and up the barn's snowy ramp.

The ammoniac warmth of the barn was welcome after the bitter cold of the past hour, and, as Rivers stepped out of the saddle, a man carrying a lantern and a pitchfork appeared out of one of the back stalls along the runway and came toward him.

"Can a man get a supper here this time of year?" Rivers asked as the other approached.

"Sure can." The man stopped a few strides away, his glance openly admiring the buckskin. "Mister, that's one hell of a sweet chunk o' horseflesh."

"He'll do." Rivers loosened the cinch. "I'll be going on after I eat. Can you give them both a good feed of grain?"

The man nodded, whereupon Rivers turned

away. He had taken two steps toward the barn's side door when he was told: "Better take that rifle and your possibles along. We got some sticky-fingered jokers hereabouts and I'll be up at the house eatin' with you."

Rivers went back to the buckskin to unleash his bedroll and take the Winchester from its scabbard, afterward leaving the barn and climbing the path to the cabin.

So it was that, some twenty minutes later, he was sitting at a big table in the cabin's cheery, lamplit kitchen with the hired man and old Stewart Bannister, owner of the station. Mag Bannister, graying and fat and genial, put a platter heaped with slices of elk roast on the table as the men turned their plates right side up. There were dumplings and stewed tomatoes and canned corn, coffee and pickles and jam and fresh-baked bread. And there were apple pies in the oven.

There was no talk as the woman joined them and they filled their plates, then fell to. Once Rivers paused long enough to say—"Ma'am, you're going to lose money on me."—his remark wreathing Mag Bannister's wrinkled face with a pleased smile.

The pie was as good as the rest of the meal, and the woman insisted on Rivers eating a second big slab, which she cut as she had the first, by quartering a pie. When Rivers had finished that and started on his second mug of coffee, he was so full he couldn't have gagged down another mouthful.

He packed his pipe and lit it as Mag Bannister began clearing the table. The hostler and Bannister were garrulously wondering if by morning they would be plowing the road higher along the pass. Neither man appeared to be paying Rivers much attention.

As he listened to the whine of the wind about the eaves beyond the kitchen window, it struck Rivers as being somewhat incongruous that he should find an old couple like the Bannisters, so patently honest and outgiving, living out their lives in such a sorry settlement as this. And presently, when the two men had talked out the subject of the probable depth of the drifts up on the pass, he picked his moment to remark: "There didn't seem to be many folks stirring about when I came up the street just now. Got the place pretty much to yourselves?"

Bannister gave his wife a wry, half-smiling glance. "It's that kind of a town. Set fire to the place and you'd flush out half a hundred of the shadiest characters in the territory. They stick by themselves and let us pretty much alone." Then, as though in apology, he added: "Wasn't like this when we came here twenty years back, though, right after the War Between the States. There was gold back in those days, not much but enough to keep the town goin'. And settlers stopping over to stay safe from the hostiles. None of this riff-raff. Why, we even had a hotel and what passed for an opera house. But then the country opened up and the business folk moved on down to the Springs. Mag and I sometimes wonder why we stay on. Guess it's because it's home."

Mag Bannister, doing the dishes at the side counter, used her apron now to wipe the soapsuds from her flabby arms, turning to look at Rivers narrowly in a way that made him sense she was sizing him up. "Pa," she said abruptly, "why don't you ask him?"

Bannister's face flushed and he avoided Rivers's eyes. "You mind your own affairs, Mag."

"But we got a right to know." Her expression was challenging, almost angry as she stared at Rivers once more, in another moment blurting out: "Would you be the man that packed Sam Cauble down off the mountain this morning?"

Frank Rivers's lean face went slack, startled at the directness and unexpectedness of the question. He took the pipe from his mouth, nodding. "I am, ma'am."

"See, I was right." The woman glanced briefly, triumphantly at her husband before asking: "What's got into that devil Pleasants? First his fence. Then trying to put the blame on a complete stranger for something he couldn't help because he happened to be riding that trail. And all this nonsense about Kate and Fred hiring you to cut fence."

Rivers shook his head, remembering now that a stage had passed him headed up the pass road shortly after he had left Ute Springs this afternoon. He supposed, and rightly, that the driver must have brought these people word of the killing and the inquest.

"It appears Pleasants is that kind," he remarked. "The kind that shoots off his mouth before he thinks a thing through."

It occurred to him that he was describing Pleasants in much the same way Kate had up there along the trail at his camp this morning. And he saw now how he could possibly steer the conversation around to his primary reason for being here. "You know the Bonds pretty well?" he asked.

"Kate and Fred?" Mag Bannister smiled wistfully. "Since before they could walk."

"Then maybe you can tell me why Pleasants is making it so hard for them. Why the fence, to begin with?"

"Because Kate jilted him," Bannister stated in no uncertain terms.

"Now, Pa, you don't know that to be a fact."

"No, but I got eyes and ears. Pleasants was squirin' Kate around all last summer. Then real quick-like he wasn't."

The woman shook her head. "No telling about that. But the fence is there, more's the pity. It was bad enough, Kate and Fred losing their folks. Now this has to happen."

"How did they lose their folks?" Rivers had wondered about this on his ride up here.

It was Bannister who answered him. "Amy and John had gone on a trip back East to visit their families in Saint Louis. They were on their way back up the Missouri on a steamer when the boilers blew. Drowned 'em, along with sixty other poor souls. We miss havin' 'em drive across here to visit like they used to."

"Is there a way across to Anchor from here?" Rivers wanted to know.

Bannister nodded. "A track cuts off to the north half a mile below town here. Takes you past Phil Crowe's line camp and straight to Anchor."

The name Bannister had mentioned gave Rivers the chance he had been waiting for, and now he drawled: "Isn't Crowe the one Fred's trying to make a deal with so as to get his beef off his range after he thins down his herd?"

The stage station owner gave his wife a surprised glance. "Hadn't heard. But if Fred's got any hope there, he can forget it. Crowe's been on the outs with Anchor for years. He'd like to see Anchor turned into a two-bit spread."

Rivers was staring vacantly down at his hands, rubbing the pipe's bowl and not liking what he was hearing. Stubbornly then, still trying to believe he had been right in the decision he had made this afternoon, he asked: "Then can't Anchor make its drive over the mountain and down to the railroad at Bend?"

Bannister sighed worriedly. "Hear that wind out there? Tonight it'll drift the peak country tight shut. And maybe there's more snow on the way." His look turned ugly then as he softly said: "Damn Pleasants and his wire."

Rivers was still arguing with himself. "Doesn't the law say a man can't close off a road with a fence? Can't the Bonds drive their beef straight down to Ute Springs along the road that leads to their layout?"

"Across Beavertail? Not the way Pleasants has rigged it," Bannister countered. "He's left the road open, sure. But his wire runs right smack along it on both sides all the way across his land. Ever try drivin' a half-wild bunch of whitefaces down a lane of barb wire? Can't be done. They'd bust the fence, get tangled in the wire, and take off every which way. Then Fred and Kate would have a lawsuit on their hands."

"Then what's the answer?"

Bannister turned his hands palms up on the table. "Prayer, maybe. Could be the good Lord'll bring on a thaw and let them drive their beef over the mountain. But at times like this a man begins to lose his faith."

"Pa, that's no way to talk."

Suddenly, and without knowing exactly what had brought about the change in him, Frank Rivers was seeing things differently.

He would pay for his supper, hit the road again. Only he was going back down through town, not over the pass. He was riding across to Anchor. There was a full moon tonight, which would make it a simple matter to find his way.

CHAPTER TEN

Phil Crowe's Pat Hand had years ago lost whatever semblance to grandeur it once possessed. It had become dingy and dirty, ill-lit and stale-aired, for Crowe was the kind of man who bothered not the slightest about neatness or any of the niceties.

The saloon's ornate mahogany bar with its heavy brass fittings hadn't once been polished since Crowe bought the place, nor had the massive and cobwebbed glass chandelier hanging from the center of the narrow room had so much as one of its miniature oil lamps dusted or lighted since the beginning of the man's tenure.

One midnight, year before last, a customer the worse off for drink had stood leaning against the bar indulging himself in some practice with a handgun. His bullets had expertly broken two arms from one side of the chandelier before Crowe somehow managed to interrupt his sport by tapping him hard across the temple with a bottle.

The chandelier still sagged to one side. And tonight Lute Pleasants, the Pat Hand's lone customer, noticed this and set his glass on the sticky counter, observing to Crowe who stood opposite him behind the front end of the bar: "You ought to wire that thing back in place. Makes the room look trashy."

"Trash is the only trade I get, so why bother?"

"Present company included?"

Crowe merely shrugged in answer. He was a gaunt, unshaven, and seedy-looking man whose tobacco-yellowed mustaches matched the habitual drooping contour of his thin lips. Tonight, as always, he wore a gray derby. And just now he reached up to push it far back on his baldpate, raising his voice to make himself heard over a wind gust rattling the street door. "So you got extra wire and posts. And three men to string fence for me. But what else?"

Pleasants, hardly knowing this man except for his reputation of being miserly and none too honest, had been expecting some such question for the past twenty minutes. So he frowned in mock puzzlement, blandly answering: "Staples, of course."

"That ain't what I mean." The saloon man lifted a hand from the counter and pointedly rubbed thumb against middle finger.

Pleasants straightened. "Cash besides?"

"What the hell do I want of a fence unless it brings me in something?"

"Brings you in something?" Pleasants echoed dryly. "Didn't I hear you once spent some time in the lockup waiting trial on a rustling charge old Bond trumped up against you? Wouldn't you like to see Anchor paid back for that, wired up there tight with no way out for their beef?"

A thin, unamused smile straightened the corners of Crowe's mouth. "Bond never knew it, but he paid plenty for what he did to me."

"And his kids are still paying for it?" Pleasants asked pointedly.

"Didn't say that," came Crowe's cautious answer. "But your fence would only be in my way unless there was some money put up besides. Look what you're . . ."

Something out on the street caught his attention then and he glanced toward the grimy window at the front of the room. The light out there was nearly gone, but Pleasants, also looking out there, saw the vague shapes of a rider and a pack animal move past and out of sight toward the lower end of town.

Instantly a hard alarm rode through him. This could be no one but Frank Rivers. And Rivers was unmistakably headed back down the cañon, not toward the pass.

"There goes your friend," Crowe unexpectedly announced.

"What friend?"

"The ranny you had the run-in with today. The one that was with Cauble when he cashed in. He come through here an hour or so ago. Headed for the pass, so I thought. Must've changed his mind."

Pleasants eyed the man narrowly, wondering

how the news of Rivers could have traveled so fast. But then he realized that Crowe, having managed so long to survive in this unsavory settlement, must have ways of hearing things. He was evidently a man of considerable though peculiar talents. It was a thing to remember.

Beavertail's owner shrugged the thought aside, saying: "Who cares? Let's get on with this other."

The saloon man was still eyeing the window in a puzzled, frowning way. And it was as though he hadn't heard Pleasants as he observed: "What's he goin' back down for when he just got here?"

Pleasants would have given a lot to have had an answer to the question. But because that was impossible, and because he was all at once anxious to be gone from here, to follow Rivers, he asked: "Where were we?"

Crowe looked around at him. "We was talkin' about a little sweetener to go with the fence." He caught Pleasants's quick shake of the head, went on: "Any day now young Bond'll be along makin' me an offer for lettin' him drive his beef down across my spread. A cash offer. I could use an extra piece of change. I need your fence about as bad as I do a mess o' silk shirts."

Pleasants slowly twirled his glass on the counter, seeming to study it as he deliberated the saloon man's ultimatum. In reality he was recalling something that had occurred to him on his way down here; he was firming it in his mind.

Crowe misread his preoccupation and made the mistake of adding: "So you got no choice."

"That so?" Pleasants glanced across obliquely at him, a spare smile breaking over his square face. "That's too bad. I figured you'd do it for just the fence."

"Nope. It'd take at least three hundred besides to make it a deal."

"Now would it?" Pleasants asked innocently. Then casually he drawled: "Well, it looks like Echols is going to have to know about those hides buried up on your place. The ones with the Anchor brands."

Crowe came bolt upright. It was as though he had been prodded with the point of a knife. His beady eyes came wider open. "Hides buried on my layout?" he echoed hollowly. "How could that be?"

The Beavertail man stood there with the fingers of his right hand idly drumming the wood. He nodded sagely. "It not only could be, it is, friend."

Crowe's beady eyes suddenly blazed with righteous anger. "By God, if there's Anchor hides buried anywhere hereabouts, you buried 'em! Any hide I ever wanted to get rid of I always burned."

"Not these, you didn't." Pleasants coolly looked the other up and down. "Of course, with all this snow a man'd have to know exactly where to dig. But that could be arranged."

"You wouldn't dare. . . ."

All at once Pleasants's square face took on a flintiness. "The hides are there, Crowe. And I know where to find them." He worded the lie baldly, bluntly. "Now does that fence go in, or doesn't it?"

The saloon man closed his eyes and shook his head as though trying to clear a fogged brain. His face had gone a pasty gray. Before he had the chance to speak, Pleasants added: "After all these years of your bleeding Anchor white, it's finally catching up with you. Unless . . ."

"You're lyin'!" Crowe burst out. "There ain't no hides!"

Pleasants shrugged. "Want to lay any bets on it?"

Crowe did an unusual thing for him then. He turned to the backbar, took down a tumbler, and reached over with trembling hands to half fill it from the bottle Pleasants had been using. Not being a drinking man, he nonetheless emptied the glass at one gulp, afterward wiping his mustaches with the back of a hand.

Yet despite the whiskey all the starch had gone out of him as he muttered lifelessly: "They'd believe it, too. Those slickers down below been wantin' all these years to saddle me with something."

"So they have." Pleasants paused, letting the words carry their weight. Then, half turning away and buttoning his coat, he said: "The boys'll move the chuck wagon and the tent across tomorrow."

The saloon owner reached up dazedly to run a palm across his damp forehead. "I heard you was a rough one to tangle with," he muttered in real bitterness. "I wish to God I'd been fifty mile from here when you showed up."

"We'll get along just fine, Crowe."

Sighing resignedly, Crowe asked: "What do I answer to folks when they want to know where I got the money to put in this damned fence? When they ask how come your crew's stringin' it for me?"

"You had an aunt die back East. She left you a stake," Pleasants answered without hesitation. "As for Ben and Harry and Red, you can say I was through with them once they finished my fence. Since they were in practice, you hired 'em."

"A hell of a likely story."

"You can improve on it maybe."

Pleasants crossed to the door now, turning up the collar of his coat as he heard the icy wind whistling along the street. About to open the door, he had a thought that made him face about and say: "Tell you what, friend. I'll even throw in the grub for your new crew. Just to show you my heart's in the right place."

"Get the hell gone," Crowe breathed explosively. "And leave the door open. The place needs airin' out."

Pleasants's booming laugh was drowned in a rush of wind as he turned out onto the snow-covered walk. His merriment lasted only briefly however, a feeling of urgency at once taking him out to his horse and making him jerk loose the knot in the reins with a vicious tug. He used the spur on the animal and was riding at a lope before he had passed the adjoining building.

Once beyond the shut-in black cañon of the street's lower end, he could begin to distinguish nearby objects with some clarity. So it was that, coming to a rutted track half a mile beyond that cut north through a timbered notch toward Crowe's line camp and Anchor, he made out along it a line of deep hoof marks trodden in the snow.

These were recent tracks, very recent, for the wind was blowing a constant whirling spume of snow that would fill in the slightest indentation within a matter of minutes.

So judging, Lute Pleasants swung into the side road. He had gone less than a hundred yards when some cautious impulse prompted him to draw the heavy .45-75 Winchester—the rifle he had used last night on Sam Cauble—from its sheath and work its lever, thus making certain that a shell was in the chamber.

Frank Rivers was almost enjoying this bitter, wild night. The moonlight made the beauty of timber and jagged ridge and snowy swale almost as dazzling as by day. He was fairly comfortable, having reversed his neckpiece and pulled it up over his nose to shield his face against the wind, and he rode most of the time with mittened hands stuffed up the sleeves of his cowhide coat. Best of all he felt warm inside.

There were times when a man had to put aside his private wants and selfishness and remember that other people's affairs counted almost as much as his own. Such was what he had felt compelled to do tonight while eating supper with the Bannisters. He wasn't in the least begrudging anyone this loss of time that interrupted his everlasting search for the lame carpenter. Anchor, or rather Kate and Fred Bond, had become important to him, oddly so, and he simply wasn't trying to analyze why he felt as he did about them.

Looking back and realizing it had been only a little more than twelve hours since he had first set eyes on Kate Bond, or even heard of Anchor, was something hard to believe. His thoughts even now were restlessly probing at possible ways the outfit could fight the awesome combination of Pleasants's new fence and this unseasonal storm. The four-month-long urgency that had kept him so constantly on the move had been replaced by another, one that strangely seemed somehow almost equally as personal.

Yesterday he had been footloose, answerable to no one but himself, calling his time his own. Now, because he wanted it this way, he was thinking of someone else for a change.

He had spent many a winter in the high country. Thinking of Anchor and what this storm might mean, he tried to look back and judge what the chances were of the weather moderating. He could remember just such a bitter spell that had prematurely struck his home range something like six years ago, when he was twenty.

It wasn't much fun. Not any, he mused.

That storm had lasted the better part of a week, as best he could recall. Then there had been a warm day or two, the snow had turned to slush, and the run-off had filled the creeks to over-flowing. The range had dried out in something like another week and he could remember that there had been almost another month of balmy autumn weather before the first real winter blizzard snowed in the range and kept it closed.

The pack mare's lagging abruptly intruded upon his thoughts and he turned in the saddle and glanced back at the animal: "Couple miles more and you can shed that load, old girl."

Hardly had his words struck against the moaning of the wind before he was seeing something moving along the white face of a low rim a little over two hundred yards obliquely behind him. At first he thought it was an elk or a deer. But then suddenly he knew that it was a man on horseback.

In another instant the rider had ghosted from sight into a heavy growth of pine capping the end of the rim. And all at once a hard alertness gripped Rivers.

"Whoever he is, he doesn't like the road."

His voice struck an alien note across a momentary stillness as the wind died away. He touched the buckskin with spur, sending the animal on at a brisker jog, his glance clinging to the ridge crest behind him. And in several more moments he imagined he saw a shadow slide quickly across an open bay of the timber close above and to his left, though afterward he couldn't be at all positive he had seen it.

Reaching down now, he drew his rifle from scabbard, levering a shell into the chamber, and then laying the weapon across the swell of the saddle, again nudging the buckskin with spur. In that brief interval he became certain that whoever it was up yonder was either anxious not to be seen or was stalking him.

The pale rosy wink of a rifle's burst all at once licked out at him from the margin of the trees barely seventy yards upward.

He felt the sharp tug of the bullet along the back of his left upper arm the instant before the explosion of a heavy rifle slapped down at him. A fierce, numbing awareness of his danger turned him rigid. He was trapped, defenseless out here in the open.

Instinctively he let his high frame go loose and off balance. Falling sideways, he cried out softly as he lost his grip on the rifle and saw it spin end over end into the snow. Then the buckskin was shying in fright, dislodging his boot from stirrup.

He went down, headfirst, very awkwardly, his face smothered in snow, his right shoulder taking his body's slamming weight. The momentum of his fall rolled him, spread-eagled, onto his back. He lay motionlessly, every nerve in him drawn wire-tight.

CHAPTER ELEVEN

Lying half buried in the snow after his ungainly fall from the buckskin, Frank Rivers held his long frame rigid against the threat of the rifle on the rim slope close above, expecting each instant to feel the slam of a second bullet into him.

Sprawled on his back at an awkward angle, his head almost covered with the powdery snow, he didn't dare move. He felt no pain whatsoever in his left arm, though he knew it had at least been grazed by the ambusher's bullet.

He had unconsciously been holding his breath, and he let it go now in a long, slow exhalation, breathing barely audibly: "Come down out of there, man. Have a look at the meat you knocked over."

There was a moment then in which a near panic ran through him at the thought of what a fool he was to be lying here, pretending to be either badly wounded or dead. Instead of gambling that the rider would come down off the ridge to make sure of his work, would come within handgun range, he was certain now that he should have cast loose the pack mare's rope and tried to make a run for it on the buckskin.

But as no sound rose over the restless whine of the bitterly cold wind, hope gradually came alive in him. It was just possible that the man up there in the timber might be convinced his bullet had squarely found its mark.

Rivers's head was tilted toward the rim, yet not far enough to let him see anything but its crest and the inky, star-studded void of the cold heavens above. Slowly, almost imperceptibly he rolled his head around until first the timber came into view, then the broken open ground sloping up to the margin of the pines. Finally he could see the buckskin and mare standing some twenty yards away, heads down and rumps turned to the icy wind.

He could feel a chill moistness and a smarting along the back of his upper left arm and knew he must be bleeding. The snow against the right side of his face, and more that had sifted down inside the collar of his coat, was gradually numbing his cheek and neck. And as his glance clung to the timber's edge, a fierce gust whipped swirling aspen leaves and a cloud of stinging snow particles into his face, chilling it to the bone.

His right leg was bent under him so that his holster painfully gouged his hips. And as the seconds slowly passed, his eyes began aching with the cold until he finally had to close them and wait until the pain eased away. When he opened his eyes to stare in the direction of the ridge again, what he saw tightened every muscle in him.

A rider was drifting slowly down out of the

blackness of the trees and toward him across the snowy open ground below.

"Keep coming," he breathed softly, prayerfully. "Move on in."

The distance between him and the ambusher was, he judged, something upward of sixty yards, too far to let him recognize who this might be, much too far for him to be certain of getting in a telling shot with the Colt.

His Winchester lay buried in the snow somewhere behind him. He briefly debated rolling over and taking his chance on finding the weapon before the rider off there could either shoot a second time or wheel back into the shelter of the timber. But then he knew he would be risking too much. He would have to lie here and play out the chance of the man coming within range of the .44.

He could plainly make out the rifle the rider held in his down-hanging right hand, and shortly he sensed the wariness of the other's approach in the way the horse angled out from a direct line and began walking a slow circle.

When the rider was passing beyond the limit of his vision, Rivers moved his head slightly. Still the man rode, coming on nearer, continuing his circle. And suddenly Rivers was faced with the threat of shortly having the man at his back, of being at the complete mercy of this killer.

That instant the tension within him built to the breaking point. He all at once threw his high frame into a convulsive roll, right hand stabbing in under coat to his holster. He plainly saw the rider stiffen, saw him begin to lift the rifle, and then jerk the reins to put his animal into a quick turn. Rivers lifted out the Colt, lined it, and squeezed off a shot. The pounding explosion of the weapon lifted a geyser of snow three feet behind the hind hoofs of the horse.

Crying out hoarsely in frustration, Rivers came to his knees as the rider bent low in the saddle and raced for the timber. He lined the Colt a second time, knew his bullet was wide of the mark as the rider swung suddenly to the right. Then a moment later the ambusher's shape was swallowed by the blackness of the timber.

Rivers stumbled across to an elongated indentation in the snow, reached down, and found the Winchester. He knocked it against the sole of his boot to clear its barrel of snow, shouldered it, and levered off three quick-timed shots aimed at the spot where the rider had disappeared. Then he snatched up his hat and ran for the buckskin.

Rage hit him then as he swung into the saddle, cast loose the pack mare's rope, and rowelled the buckskin with spur, running toward the trees at the foot of the rim. He came to the line of the ambusher's tracks and followed them into the trees at a hard run. But then he was riding in a gray twilight, the snowy ground ahead a shadowless blanket that showed not a mark, not a track.

He put the buckskin between the pines and through the thickets of buckbrush and scrub oak with a savage and reckless abandon, trusting the animal's sure-footedness. Then suddenly he rode out into bright moonlight once more, cresting the rim.

Swinging quickly to his left, he rode for two hundred yards, studying the drifted expanse of ground ahead of him, using his free hand to shield his face from the wind-whipped snow. He found no tracks and finally, impatiently turned about and ran back the way he had come. A like distance from the point where he had gained the ridge crest he came across a line of tracks that topped the broken ground and angled down its far side into another growth of pine.

He had followed the tracks almost down to the trees when he finally began listening to a voice of caution that somehow made itself heard over the cold rage seething in him: "Easy now. Let's think this over."

The sound of his voice served to steady him, to make him see that he was being foolhardy and acting without any judgment whatsoever. When he came to the margin of the pines, he reined in, hearing nothing but the whine of the wind through the tops of the trees and, in the distance, the eerie howl of a night-hunting wolf.

Over the next several seconds he understood that he couldn't go on. The ambusher would either keep on going or would choose his spot for making a second try at him. If the man chose to run, it was a hopeless chore tracking him. If he chose to make another try at bringing down the quarry he had missed, then there was no possible way of Rivers guessing when he might be riding into a trap.

"But who was he?" His voice was rough-edged with anger and bafflement. "Who'd be after me?"

As he sat there, scanning the deep shadows of the timber below, he felt a chill moistness along the back of his left hand. Looking at the hand, he saw a streak of blood lined down from wrist to the tip of his index finger. Only then was he aware of a painful smarting along the back of his upper arm, and of his sleeve being wet.

He came down out of the saddle, took off his coat, and rolled up the sleeve of his shirt to see plainly that the bullet had channeled a trough a half inch deep at the back of the ropey muscle of his upper arm. It was bleeding, and he unknotted his neckpiece and bound it about the arm, feeling the knifing chill of the night now and all at once impatient to be on his way to Anchor.

Once he had pulled on his coat, he rode back over the ridge and down through the trees to the road. The mare was standing where he had left her.

He wasted no time in gathering up her rope and heading on along the road, his glance ceaselessly roving his back trail as he angrily tried to puzzle out the enigma of this past quarter hour.

CHAPTER TWELVE

Lute Pleasants had been as certain of his .45-75 having found its mark as he had been last night when using the weapon on Sam Cauble. He had therefore been panicked when Frank Rivers rolled over in the snow to throw that first shot at him.

The hollow explosions of Rivers's .44 had made him punish his horse in climbing the ridge, and afterward the slapping thunder of the rifle searching for him made him frantically swing to one side as he cut up through the pines. He had paused briefly below the crest of the rim to glance back down through the trees and could see Rivers running for the buckskin. And afterward he had topped the rim and ridden down its far side, wanting nothing so much as to put distance between him and the man he had tried to kill.

The high alarm that gripped Pleasants made him think of but one thing, getting out of there. He rode on as fast as the horse would carry him, making brief changes in direction, working his way west and lower across the hills. Once, after covering perhaps a mile, he stopped beyond the crest of a rise and delayed half a minute, scanning his back trail. He saw nothing moving across the upward distance, and, when he went on, enough of the gnawing fear had left him to allow him to think back upon the quirk of circumstance that had so suddenly changed his luck from good to bad.

When the full realization came of what a fool he had been in not simply putting another bullet into Rivers, he relieved his feelings in much the same way he had yesterday after his run-in with Sam Cauble. His raging outburst of obscene oaths startled his horse, made the animal shy and toss its head.

That, more than any inward prompting, stifled Pleasants's rage and made him begin to consider what he was to do next. First of all, he must hide his sign so thoroughly that no one tonight or tomorrow could possibly track him. The wind would help, and with that knowledge he set about the task methodically and thoroughly.

Yet, as he put the miles behind him, the rancor in him didn't die away. It was plain to him that Frank Rivers must have reconsidered Fred Bond's offer of a job with Anchor, that the man was probably already at the ranch by now. So it was that his thoughts began coupling Anchor with Rivers.

It was perhaps half an hour later that he was suddenly struck by an idea that immediately made him change his direction and swing into the north. And in forty more minutes he was climbing into the higher hills once more in the direction of his new fence.

By the time he sighted the dying fire at the fence camp, he was tired and chilled to the bone. He rode in past the half dozen animals in the rope corral below the big tent and gave a shout as he came in on the burned-down blaze.

Ben Galt was the first man to make an appearance. By that time Pleasants was at the fire, throwing on wood to build up the blaze. Galt had pulled his pants on over heavy underwear and stood, peering sleepily from the tent flap as he stepped into his boots.

"Rout out Harry and Red," Pleasants told him. "We've got work to do."

"Tonight?"

"Tonight. Now. Hurry it up."

Galt grunted in disgust and disappeared inside the tent. Shortly he came out, pulling on his shirt, holding hat and coat as he strode across to the fire. "Where to, boss?"

"Wait'll the others get here," was Pleasants's gruff answer.

He emptied the coffee grounds from a tin cup he saw lying alongside the fire and filled the cup from a blackened pot sitting at the edge of the coals. He was downing the lukewarm liquid when first Harry Blake, then Red Majors, came out of the tent.

"Tonight's the night we've been waiting for," he unceremoniously told the three. "We haul that scoop through the fence and up across Anchor to a big cut where the creek splits. You three're so new here you don't know the spot, but I can find the way. With this freeze, the creek'll be low. We'll have maybe four hours to dig the bed of our branch deeper and get out before it gets light. You'd better wear plenty of clothes."

Ben Galt was frowning, plainly not liking this but nonetheless hardly disposed to argue it, though he did mutter: "It's killin' cold to be workin' in water."

"Chances are the creek will only be running a trickle," Pleasants told him, quickly adding: "Another thing. Tomorrow you're moving camp across onto Crowe's place. To put in fence for him." He was enjoying their startled expressions as he went on: "You'll be with him for maybe a month, then come back to finish up for me."

"Crowe's good for the money?" Galt wanted to know.

"He'd better be. He's given me his word on it, which is why I'm doing him the favor of loaning you to him."

Red Majors's broad face shaped a slow grin. "Sounds good. I can use the extra cash."

"Then let's get goin'," Ben Galt said, turning toward the tent.

Harry, following him, drawled morosely: "Listen to that wind. Better put on every damn' thing you own. She's goin' to be cripplin' cold before we're finished."

CHAPTER THIRTEEN

B y the second afternoon following the inquest, the holding grounds to the south of Ute Springs was crowded with upward of five hundred head of bawling, hungry cattle. Almost every outfit for thirty miles around, spooked by the storm, was shipping ahead of time. Yet the weather made all this bustle and hurry seem a trifle incongruous, for it was sunny and warm and thawing as it had yesterday. It was a perfect, balmy autumn afternoon.

Jim Echols sat the top rail of a loading pen near a chute where a boxcar was being loaded with prime steers. He hadn't bothered to wear a coat, and the sun felt good on his back.

The pens were deeply mired with mud. Water lay everywhere. The last of the snow was going fast and Squaw Creek, a hundred yards to the west, roared with the run-off.

The lawman held a tally board across one knee and penciled a mark on a sheet of paper as each animal was urged with prod pole up the slippery cleats to the ramp and into the boxcar. Up ahead the locomotive's compressor wheezed idly while the engineer leaned out of his cab window awaiting the brakeman's signal to move the freight ahead along the siding so as to load the next empty boxcar.

Echols idly noticed a team pulling a buckboard through the mud toward him along this near side of the pens, though he didn't recognize the driver until the rig had pulled to a stop below him and Fred Bond called: "Got a minute, Jim?"

The sheriff glanced down, saying cheerfully: "Look who's here. Be with you as soon as we finish this car."

In two more minutes he hung the tally board from a nail on the pen's corner post and swung down to the next-to-bottom rail, stepping across to the wheel hub, and easing onto the buckboard's seat. "Thought you'd be too busy to hit town again this soon."

"Came in after a load of salt," Fred told him. "On the way back I'm taking the long way around. To see Crowe."

Echols brows lifted. "Hopin' for any luck with him?"

Fred Bond smiled crookedly. "Not any. But at least I can try."

"And if he won't let you drive across his place?"

"Then we'll go up and over the mountain. It just might work. The snow's going off fast even up there." Over a slight hesitation, Fred added: "But that wasn't what I came to tell you."

At the lawman's questioning look, Fred decided to be blunt about his reason for being here. "Now wait'll you hear what I have to say before you blow up, Jim. It's this. Frank Rivers has taken that job I offered him."

The sheriff's head came up. His stare took on a stoniness. "I told that joker to clear out and keep goin'."

"I know, I know. But he saw what a spot we were in and decided we needed help. That isn't what matters, though. What does is that someone took a shot at him on his way across from Summit night before last."

Jim Echols's expression briefly mirrored complete astonishment. "Anyone with him to prove his story?"

"No, but . . ."

The lawman's low, mocking laugh cut Fred short. "Then why swallow it? He's a one for makin' up a fancy tale."

Fred was finding it hard to keep a rein on his patience as he said: "There's this much proof. Collins and I were out on the meadow forking hay from the stacks. We heard a shot, what we thought was a rifle away off in the distance. Then three or four minutes later there were more, five altogether. As it turned out, it was Rivers. He'd been caught out in the open. So he hit the ground and played 'possum. Tolled this gent almost down to him, then had the bad luck to miss him with his Forty-Four, then with his rifle. Whoever it was hit the brush fast and kept going." He eyed Echols solemnly, adding: "He's got a chunk ripped out the back of his arm deep enough to lay your thumb in, Jim. Now I suppose you'll say he probably shot himself."

The edge of sarcasm in those words wasn't lost on the sheriff, who sat a long moment in thought before soberly asking: "Where'd this happen?"

"Off near Sawmill Ridge, as near as we can make out."

"Does Rivers know who it was?"

"No."

The blast of the locomotive's exhaust took the lawman's attention now. A rattle of couplings sounded over the bawling of the cattle and the freight began crawling ahead, whereupon Echols turned on the seat and called to a rider inside the pen: "Mose, get up here and spell me with the tally on this load, will you?"

The rider nodded and headed for the pen gate, whereupon the sheriff settled back on the seat and glanced at Fred again, his look quite grave. "What's Rivers's idea on this?"

Fred Bond shook his head. "He doesn't have one. But I do. Someone's out to get him. Half a hand spread to the front and that chunk of lead would have made him a meal for the lobos."

Echols was completely baffled and showed that now as he gave a long, whistling sigh, drawling dourly: "First Cauble, now Rivers. Can't make head or tail of it."

"Look at it this way, Jim. Suppose you're wrong

and Frank is right about his pardon. Suppose the word's got around that he's hunting the sidewinders that cut down his father? Suppose they've heard of it and are hunting him?"

The lawman lifted a hand in a deprecatory gesture. "That's askin' too much of a man to believe."

Fred shrugged. "Well, you know about Frank now, anyway. And I'd thank you to keep hands off him at least until we're out of the woods. Yesterday he did as much work as any other two men could've, even with the bad arm. He and Collins and I cleaned out those finger draws up to the east of the layout. Today he's working the north bench with Kate. Give us four or five more good days and we'll be ready to move our beef down. Or"—he added dryly—"move it up."

Jim Echols took out tobacco and papers and built a smoke, scowling down at his hands, afterward offering Fred the makings. Fred shook his head, whereupon the sheriff licked his cigarette, shaped it, and only then said: "All right, it's your look-out who you hire. I'll keep hands off. But after you're through with this, I want that man to get the hell clear of here and stay away." Acid in his tone, he concluded: "If you'd ever known Bill Echols like he once was and could see him now, you'd understand why I don't want that lanky moose around."

"Anything you say, Jim." Fred was mightily relieved.

Frank and Kate had boiled their coffee over a small fire at midday and had eaten a quick, cold meal of bread and jerky, Kate afterward heading back down toward Anchor's main meadow driving forty-odd head of cattle, their morning's gather.

Now, with the sun beginning to dip toward the far horizon, Frank's three hours of being on his own had netted him only five steers and three heifers as he worked down out of a box cañon, pushing the cattle ahead of him. The buckskin's hoofs occasionally kicked up a fine spray of muddy water, and the sodden drifts were melting fast, with large patches of steaming bare ground showing here and there. Another day like this would see most of the snow gone except for that along the shadowed northern slopes.

The memory of the rifle shot that had so narrowly missed killing him night before last was still strong in Frank. His arm was stiff and sore, all but useless. Yesterday and today he had ridden warily. Numerous times he had unobstrusively climbed to high ground and spent long minutes scanning the surrounding hills and the open pockets in the timber, looking for some furtive movement of man or animal that might warn him of someone stalking him. So far he had found absolutely nothing to reward his alertness.

Many times he had deliberately tried to think out the answer to the riddle of who might have taken the shot at him. At first it seemed highly probable that someone he had met over the past four months—possibly someone who begrudged him his pardon—had followed him to this out-of-the-way spot. But, with the exception of Jim Echols, he could recall no one who bore him enough real animosity to want to take his life.

He had even soberly considered the possibility of Echols's having been the man there along the rim two nights ago. But instinct rebelled against this. The sheriff might heartily dislike him, even loathe him for what had happened to Bill Echols. Yet he judged it wasn't in Echols's make-up to force himself to the act of committing outright murder.

His reaction to the thought of Lute Pleasants being the guilty party had been much the same. In the beginning, up there at his camp along the trail, he realized that the Beavertail man's high rage might have driven him to shooting to kill. But afterward, when Pleasants had had the chance to think over the circumstances surrounding Cauble's death, the man's common sense had outweighed that original rash impulse. It seemed beyond the realm of reason that Pleasants, after his about-face at the inquest, could have had any interest whatsoever in the luckless stranger who had had the misfortune to be a witness to the killing of his foreman.

Never, not even when he had been arrested for the murder of his father, had Frank Rivers been confronted with an enigma so completely baffling as this. Only one thing had occurred to him that made any sense at all, a possibility he had talked over last night with Kate and Fred. This was the likelihood that somehow the word that he was hunting down the two men who had robbed the Peak City stage had reached those two and that they were in turn hunting him.

If this could be so, if it was one of that pair who had taken the shot at him, then it might mean that his weeks and months of futile searching were nearly at an end. Today he had thought much of this, fervently hoping that it might be so.

Just now, as he rode out of the wide mouth of the cañon, he was startled at finding Kate waiting for him close below alongside a clump of alders flanking the stream that snaked down from his high bench to wind out across Anchor's big head-quarters meadow, four miles distant. He hadn't expected to see Kate again until suppertime, and now the prospect of being with her filled him with a sense of well-being that at once lightened the somberness of his thoughts.

"Think we ought to send for help to handle these?" he asked as he rode in on her, nodding to the eight animals drifting off along the stream.

Kate laughed. "That's why I'm here. Collins just told me he and Fred worked that box and everything north of here last week. Thought I'd better go back and tell you."

Frank folded his arms and leaned on the horn of the saddle. "So where to now?"

"Down to the fence. Collins thinks the storm may have pushed a few of the wild ones in on the wire."

She turned as she spoke, gathered up her gelding's reins, and stepped into the saddle, then led the way up along the edge of the thicket and, beyond it, swung in toward the creek.

Frank, following, took in the sureness with which her willowy upper body kept its straight-backed balance when the gelding stumbled once as a small rock turned under hoof. There was a quality of grace, of physical well-being about this girl that oddly went hand in hand with a certain mischievousness and lightheartedness he had discovered in her yesterday in strong contrast to her seriousness the day of the inquest.

It struck him suddenly that he had never before been so intrigued by a woman, nor found one so volatile and at the same time so straightforward and steadfast as Kate Bond. And there was a deep humility in him as he realized how completely she seemed to trust him. So far as he had been able to discover, she believed in him, in the justice of his pardon, and in his reasons for being here.

She turned in the saddle now, looking back and smiling as she asked: "How's the arm? Stiff?"

"Better," he told her.

He had answered almost absent-mindedly, for they were coming in on the grassy bank of the stream and a moment ago he had seen something that whetted his curiosity.

Kate noticed his preoccupation and drew rein, waiting for him to come in alongside her. Then, as though she could almost read his thoughts, she asked: "What is it, Frank?"

He nodded on ahead to where the muddy water rippled along the rocky bed of the stream well below the level of the grassy banks. "Doesn't this run much water except after a storm?"

The question made her stare at him in strong puzzlement. "Of course it does. Why Fred catches trout out of . . ." Her words trailed off and her eyes came wider open as she abruptly caught the point of his question. "It should be deeper, shouldn't it? Because of the run-off. A lot deeper."

He nodded. "A lot."

Kate looked upstream toward the higher hills to the north out of which the creek found its way. "Something's blocked it, Frank." Her glance betrayed a strong exasperation then. "This would have to happen right now, when we've got twice as much as we can do anyway."

"A slide's probably changed the channel," Frank told her. "Want to follow it on up and have a look?"

"We'll have to. It wouldn't be so funny if it runs dry next week after all this snow's gone."

She impatiently reined the gelding on out and along the line of the stream, Frank putting the buckskin in alongside her. And in another two minutes, when he saw that her worried frown hadn't thinned, he drawled: "Ten to one some brush or logs have dammed it. Can't be anything a stick of giant powder couldn't blow loose."

"Let's hope so. Just thinking of losing what water we have makes me turn cold inside."

"Who said you were losing it?"

"I know we're not." Kate forced a smile. "But for a minute there I got to wondering what it would be like if we did. It would . . . it could be the end of Anchor."

She spurred the gelding into a quicker jog then and they rode for another mile without speaking, meantime angling up off the bench and riding between a series of rocky, timbered hills. Once, rounding a bend in the stream, they came upon a buck and three doe and watched them bound away into the towering pines. Another time they surprised two bald eagles feeding upon the carcass of a yearling, and, as they climbed higher between the shadowed hills, Frank could feel the heat going out of the day.

The creek, he noticed, had shallowed and was running only a fraction of the volume it had below. Finally they came to the mouth of a cliff-hemmed cut too narrow to let them follow the stream except by wading their animals up along its rocky channel.

Kate drew rein, looking across and up a trail that climbed the rocky slope of the gorge's west wall. "There's the only way around this stretch," she impatiently told Frank. "It's at least two more miles to the forks."

"The forks?"

"Yes. Where the Porcupine splits. We call this branch Owl Creek. The Porcupine drops down across Beavertail and empties into the Squaw six or seven miles above town."

"Then let's get at it." Frank led the way across the shallowing stream to the twisting trail and started up along it.

They took the better part of a quarter of an hour climbing a series of switchbacks to the rim. And at the head of the trail Frank looked east across the gorge to see a series of snow-splotched and timbered hills climbing all the upward distance to the boulder fields below the lofty, whitened peaks.

Rarely had he gazed upon such lush summer range. And as Kate joined him he breathed in genuine awe: "So this is what Pleasants passed up for his fence."

"It is."

She gave him a sidelong, speculative glance, debating something that shortly made her ask:

"You've been wondering about that, haven't you?"

He looked around at her. "About what, Kate?"

"Why he hates us so much that he'd put in the fence."

He halfway grasped that what she was about to say was in dead seriousness. Nodding slowly, he drawled: "Guess I have."

"It's because of me, Frank. I . . . Lute and I saw a lot of each other last summer. He was . . . he can be very nice when it suits him. He was always that way with me."

When she hesitated, he looked away, faintly embarrassed at having prompted her to speak of something so personal. Yet as she went on her voice was firmer, her tone edged with real anger. "He was until one particular day. That day I saw him for what he really is. He was riding a half-broken horse, a paint. The horse shied and nearly threw him. He must have forgotten I was there. Because he flew into a rage that . . . that is still hard to believe. He got down and picked up a stick, a club. He was beating the horse about the head when I stopped him."

Kate was pale, her voice trembled. "I cut him across the face with the ends of my reins. I called him things . . . things a man would have called him." Her head came up and there was a defiant look in her eyes. "I told him he was a coward, that I never wanted to have anything to do with him again, not ever. There was something about him right then that made me as afraid as I've ever been."

As she stopped speaking, Frank whistled softly. "Let him have his fence. You and Fred are going to lick this thing."

"I wonder. Night before last, the night you came, I suppose I was desperate. Sam Cauble's dying had made me realize what a serious thing this is. I offered to go down to Lute and beg him to let us take our cattle out across Beavertail. Fred wouldn't listen."

"I don't blame him."

She gave him a look of gratitude. "So that's the story, Frank. We're going to do the best we can. And we're doing it without Lute's help."

She abruptly spurred ahead of him and led the way on along the rim, Frank soberly thinking back over what she had said with a degree of awe at realizing how willingly she had taken him into her confidence.

As they went on, they now and then rode the chill, silent corridor of a stand of spruce or golden aspen, at other times threaded their way through mazes of rotten outcroppings. Occasionally they swung over to the rim's edge and looked down across the two-hundred foot drop to the stream foaming whitely along its rocky bed far below.

Frank noticed that the stream had diminished even more in its flow, though he made no mention of that as they went steadily on. And shortly Kate told him: "We'll have to give this up in another half mile or so when we come to the forks."

They covered that distance in ten more minutes, abruptly riding out onto a promontory that jutted like the prow of a ship and sloped steeply down to mark the dividing point where the upper stream separated into its two channels. To the right was the twisting line of the Owl Creek gorge they had been following, to the left lay a shorter slot soaking through the lower hills to mark the falling course of the Porcupine.

Kate was in the lead as they came to the rim's edge. She peered downward and Frank saw her stiffen, then turn quickly and motion him to join her, giving him a wide-eyed and incredulous stare.

He rode in alongside her and looked down into the gorge that lay in deep shadow. For a moment he failed to see what had so startled her. But then all at once he made out several long, straight criss-crossed furrows of bare earth down there patterned blackly against the whiteness of the unmelted snow blanketing the banks of both branches of the stream.

The Porcupine was full to overflowing. Its booming roar sounded up plainly to them as it raced along its channel. On the near side of that channel ran a straight, high mound of freshly turned gravel, blocking all but a trickle of water from the branching that led into the Owl Creek gorge.

"It's a dam," Kate breathed. "Who would . . . ?" Her face had gone pale. Now suddenly her eyes brightened in fury. "Lute!" she cried softly. "It couldn't be anyone else!"

A core of anger was hardening in Frank. He said nothing, though he was already halfway grasping the cunning that lay behind the work that had been done down there. What struck him hardest of all was that, except for this unforeseen thaw, the blocking of Owl Creek channel might never have been discovered.

"What do we do, Frank?" Kate's voice was unsteady, the look she gave him an awed, furious one. "Bring Jim Echols up here and show it to him?"

"Let's have a look." Frank reined the buckskin over to a point on the rim fifty yards away that let him look down on the upper reach of the Porcupine, stepped out of the saddle. By the time Kate stood beside him he had seen enough down there to let him tell her: "There's the way they came. Looks like the tracks of a sled. They did the work with a scoop and a team."

"Jim is going to see this. And I'm going to have it out with Lute. We can haul him into court for this."

Frank gave her a glance that was faintly amused. "Suppose our friend says he doesn't know anything about this? Suppose he . . . ?"

"But who else could have done it?"

Frank nodded. "It probably was Pleasants. But where's your proof? He can say it was someone else that wanted to make trouble between your two outfits. Then there's this. Down below, where the sun has had a chance at the snow, you're not going to find any sled tracks. He's in the clear, Kate."

"But Jim Echols can see it with his own eyes. He'll know."

"Sure. But even that's not proof enough to bring before a court."

His words heightened her look of helplessness and bafflement, and in another moment she was asking in a small voice: "Then what can we do?"

He hesitated in his answer, peering below once more. This rim on which they stood sloped steeply downward in a series of rotten sandstone ledges and talus slopes all the way to the narrow banks along the channel of the Porcupine. Fifty yards farther along the rim rose a thirty-foot-high formation of shelf rock that was badly weathered, its inner edge crumbling away.

Slabs of sandstone had fallen from the table rock's side and lay close to the edge of the rim, some upended and lying against others. And directly beyond a thin stand of aspen grew along the line of the drop-off, a few of the trees leaning precariously outward and hanging by their roots where portions of the rim had fallen away.

Sight of those exposed tree roots all at once

roused a thought in Frank that was like suddenly being able to see clearly in total darkness. He looked around at Kate with a glance that mirrored a genuine awe, drawling: "What can you do?" He nodded toward the slabs of rock lying so close to the edge of the drop-off. "There's your way of making friend Pleasants wish he'd never come up here."

For a long moment Kate's expression was one of complete mystification. Then abruptly a look of dawning comprehension brought her eyes wider open. She quickly moved a step closer to the rim and peered downward. When her glance finally came around to Frank again, her green eyes were bright with a blend of excitement and alarm.

"You're trying to tell me we could block off the Porcupine?"

"Yes. So tight nothing could ever blow it loose. But," he added gravely, "you've got to think what it would mean to Anchor, all that water pouring out across your range."

"What does it mean to Beavertail?" Kate countered. "It means grass, a world of it."

"Another thing," he said still speaking very seriously. "Suppose Pleasants comes up here and finds our tracks? He can . . ."

"Suppose he does?" she cut in, fire in her eyes now. "Would he dare tell Echols? Or anyone else? You and I have seen what he's done down there."

She turned quickly away then, hurrying across to

the base of the towering formation of sandstone, looking around once and calling impatiently: "Come on, Frank!"

He smiled as he followed her, some of the same excitement that was gripping her beginning to have its way with him now. And as he joined her, he said: "Woman, I'd hate ever to be on the outs with you."

"You're not Lute Pleasants, so you probably never will be." She walked across to a tilted-up slab of sandstone close to the edge of the rim, telling him—"This one will do for a start."—bending down to get a grip on its lower edge.

He joined her, leaned over, and took a handhold close beside her, breathing—"Now."—and putting all his strength into the lift. A stab of pain ran up along his bad arm, yet he ignored it, feeling the touch of Kate's shoulder against his as the muscles of her slender body tensed.

The rock was very heavy, four feet long and a foot in thickness, though narrow. He felt it inch upward and threw more of his weight behind it. And as it tilted farther, he rasped out: "Back, Kate."

She didn't move, didn't say anything. And as he felt the rock all at once tilt beyond the vertical and begin its outward fall, he threw an arm about her waist, wheeled, and ran back from the edge of the rim.

Ten strides took them back past the base of

the table rock, Kate meantime gripping Frank's hand and holding it tighter about her waist in sudden fright at a rumbling sound rising out of the gorge behind them. They stopped and turned then, facing the rim as the rumble mounted to a low roar.

They could feel the earth trembling under them, and off to their right the buckskin whickered in sudden panic. The roar gathered volume until it drowned out the sound of the stream far below. Dust began rising lazily out of the depths.

Where they had been standing only seconds ago, a twenty-foot stretch of the rim all at once tilted outward and vanished from sight, taking four aspen trees with it. They heard that heavy mass of rimrock strike a shelf below with a prolonged, hollow booming that echoed back from the far wall of the gorge. And across there Frank was amazed to see a wedge of talus all at once move slowly downward and settle out of sight in a smother of dust.

He called above the roar—"Let's get out of here!"—and pushed Kate on ahead of him and farther back from the rim.

They ran across to the buckskin and gelding, quieting the animals as the last low rumble of falling rock echoed up out of the depths.

Kate looked at Frank, her face pale, her expression aghast. "Can we . . . can we look now?"

He nodded, and she came quickly across to him, reaching out and taking his hand, needing the assurance of his physical presence to steady her as they walked slowly out to the rim's edge.

As she peered downward, she clenched his hand so tightly that her nails bit into his palm. Yet he didn't feel that in his awe at what he was seeing through the settling pall of dust down there.

The gorge of the Porcupine was choked to a height of a third of its depth by a peaked dam of rock and rubble. The stream was already backing up behind it, forming a small lake.

In another quarter hour, Frank supposed, Lute Pleasants's dam across the mouth of the Owl would be washed away and the gorge below it roaring with the full force of the run-off.

CHAPTER FOURTEEN

They had little to say on the long ride back from the rim, both of them awed to silence by what they had witnessed up there.

For they had waited to see the roiled waters of the Porcupine slowly fill in behind the awesome mound of the slide to form a small lake littered with débris—branches, a few logs, and floating yellow islands of aspen and willow leaves. Then, as though it had been built as a plaything for the amusement of a child, the seething waters had burst over Lute Pleasants's carefully built gravel dam and washed it away.

The near end of the dam still remained. "Something you can show Echols," Frank had said. And as they rode on down along the line of the gorge, the booming roar of the stream coursing down the bed of the Owl had been a muted thunder following them.

Twilight lay across the mile-long meadow and its fenced stacks of wild timothy as they rode down on Anchor. No light showed in either the bunkhouse windows or those of the sprawling house of square-cut logs, and Kate had finally ended a long interval of silence by saying: "Wade always works till it's too dark to see. And we needn't count on Fred being here for supper. He may be spending more time with Crowe than he'd planned on."

They had rounded the far end of the barn and were riding in on the corral at the near end of the pasture when Frank abruptly noticed the buckboard blocking the corral gate alongside the watering trough, the team standing, heads down, patiently waiting.

It was the rig Fred had driven to town this morning. Something about the look of it—perhaps the fact of the reins being wound about the brake arm—sent its sharp warning to him. Something was wrong here, very wrong.

The light was so poor that he hoped Kate hadn't noticed the buckboard yet. As casually as he could, he told her: "Some coffee would go down good right now. Go on up to the house . . ."

"Fred's back," she cut in, not giving him the chance to finish what he had been about to say. "But why would he leave the team that way?"

He left her side then, putting the buckskin over there at a lope. He came in alongside the buckboard and looked down into it, caught his breath.

Fred Bond lay sprawled on his back between several disarranged blocks of salt. His face was puffed, swollen. His eyes were closed, his head rolled around to the side. Blood stained his mouth and the boards below his head.

Frank wheeled on away and back out to meet Kate. He caught her gelding's reins, pulled the animal to a halt, saying tonelessly: "Get on up to the house, Kate."

CHAPTER FIFTEEN

Forty minutes after he had carried Fred Bond to his bedroom at Anchor, helped Kate undress him, and listened to his sometimes incoherent story, Frank Rivers rode his badly blown buckskin up Ute Springs' main street to Doc Lightfoot's house.

Within three minutes of knocking on the medico's door, he was helping Lightfoot hitch a mare to a buggy they had pushed out of a shed to the rear of the house.

"Tell me about that arm again," the doctor said as he climbed into the buggy and unwound the reins from the whip socket. "Could he move it? Was there a break?"

"No break we could find. We had to straighten it. Then's when he yelled and went under."

"Dislocation then. Hurts to beat hell."

"Doc"—Frank waited until the medico, turning the buggy, reined in and looked down at him once more—"it may be Fred's hurt bad. So get up there fast as this mare'll take you. If you kill her getting you there, I'll see you get another."

"Don't worry, I'll make tracks." Lightfoot's voice was low-pitched in anger over what he had heard these past two minutes. "And just remember, Fred's tough."

He drove out the yard gate then and turned down the street, the mare at a fast trot. Frank trudged on out past the house and to the buckskin tied at a rail beyond the walk, beginning to feel his tiredness now. He stood there until the buggy's lamps had faded from sight around a bend far below, the quiet rage still seething in him as he thought back on those ten minutes he had spent with Fred before leaving Anchor.

Kate's brother, he supposed, would never be quite the same again. The arm might heal and be all right, and many a man had got along without three of his teeth. But no man, regardless of his disposition, could keep from becoming in some degree bitter after being beaten about the head with a gun, after being booted in chest and stomach and groin until sheer agony dragged him into unconsciousness.

He thought—*Now Echols.*—with an added measure of resentment. About to climb to the saddle again, he decided against it and, grateful for the way the buckskin had carried him down here, reached over to slap the animal gently on the neck, afterward taking a hold on the reins and leading him on up the street.

Not a window in the courthouse showed a light, so he walked on as far as the livery, let the buckskin drink briefly from the street trough, then led him into the barn and put him in a stall. He took off the saddle, paid the hostler for two measures of oats and one of corn, and only then asked: "Where would a man find Echols this time of night?"

"Jim? No tellin'. Try at the hotel."

Frank went on up the street and shortly cut across it toward the lights of the hotel, wondering about the reception the sheriff would give him if he could find him. As he climbed the verandah steps leading to the Hill House's entrance, the tantalizing odor of cooking meat from a restaurant two doors below made him suddenly realize he was ravenous. But that didn't matter just yet.

Inside, he crossed the lamplit lobby to a counter at the foot of the stairway, asking the old man behind it: "Jim Echols been around tonight?"

The other nodded to a broad doorway on the far side of the room. "He ought to be right in there, eating his supper."

Frank saw Echols the moment he stepped to the entrance of the nearly empty dining room. The lawman was eating at a table in the far corner in company with a young woman with a freckled, plain-looking face and straw-colored hair.

Uneasy over having to intrude upon this somehow intimate scene and interrupt the sheriff's meal, Frank nevertheless took off his hat and walked across there. Jim Echols happened to look up and see him coming, and a scowl settled over his thin face.

"If you're here to see me, I'm busy," he brusquely remarked as Frank reached the table.

His tone ruffled Frank's unsteady temper. Yet Frank managed to say quietly: "Fred Bond's taken a bad beating. Doc Lightfoot's on his way out to see him. Thought you ought to know about it."

The lawman's look of truculence vanished before one of undisguised apprehension. "Fred hurt? Who did it?"

Frank glanced pointedly down at the girl. "Hadn't we better step outside?"

Echols misread his meaning and snapped: "Lola's to be trusted. Come on, man, out with it."

Deciding to match the other's bluntness, Frank shrugged meagerly, saying: "They knocked out three of his teeth, cut up his face and head. They may've kicked in a couple ribs. Something's wrong with his left arm and . . ."

"Who the hell was it?" the sheriff burst out, his thin face pale now, his voice grating in bridled anger that wasn't directed at Frank.

"Three Beavertail men, Harry and Ben and one other. Only now they claim they're working for a man named Crowe."

"For Phil Crowe?" The lawman's look mirrored outright incredulity. "Doing what?"

"Putting in more fence." Frank waited a moment for Echols to take this in, then went on: "Fred had been across to see Crowe in Summit when . . ."

"I know all that. He told me today he was goin' to see Crowe. Where'd this happen, in Summit?"

"No. Right at the line between Crowe's land and

Anchor. They've set up a camp down below and started digging post holes. They spotted Fred on his way home, stopped him, said they'd hired on with Crowe, and that he was to keep to his side of the line from here out. He lost his head and admits he started the argument."

"Which means my hands are tied." The lawman sighed in disgust and glanced at Lola Ames to say wearily: "What was I tellin' you about bein' over a barrel? First the fence, then that Cauble mess. Now this. What's a man to do? Where do I start from to set things right?"

The girl had been plainly ill at ease during this heated interchange. Now she abruptly pushed her chair back and rose from the table. "I'd better . . . I'll leave you two alone."

Echols came awkwardly to his feet, protesting: "But you haven't finished eatin' yet."

"Never mind, Jim." There was a surprising quality of firmness in the girl's tone. She looked up at Frank, smiling unexpectedly, warmly. "Mister Rivers, I don't happen to agree with Jim on everything. He's told me about your staying to help Kate and Fred. No matter what he thinks, I . . . well, I'm glad you did."

Her face taking on color as she realized how outspoken she'd been, Lola turned quickly and left them then, crossing the room and going out into the lobby.

Her words had their effect on Jim Echols. For as

he spoke again now his tone was for the first time quite mild: "You look beat, Rivers. Had your supper yet?"

At Frank's shake of the head, he motioned to the chair the girl had just vacated. "Then have a seat. We can order you a meal."

Frank was thoroughly taken aback by this abrupt change in the man's manner. He would have liked nothing better than to do what Echols was suggesting, yet the memory of the sheriff's contempt and loathing for him wasn't to be this easily brushed aside. For an instant he groped for a sarcastic way of saying as much, but then suddenly knew it wouldn't be worth it.

Shrugging mentally, he said only: "Kate'll be expecting me back at the place."

Echols's look just then was confused, uneasy, as though he knew what Frank had been thinking. And he hurried to ask: "What's Kate goin' to do about this?"

"I don't think she's decided yet. It's hit her pretty hard."

"'Course it has." Frowning worriedly, the lawman added: "Fred stopped by to see me today. Told me you ran into some lead the other night. How's the arm?"

"Coming along fine." Frank wanted nothing so much as to get out of here now, and went on: "There's one more thing you ought to know. Kate and I were working the hills off to the north of the layout today. This afternoon we happened to notice that the creek was low, even with the snow going so fast. So we rode on up to see what was blocking it. We had to go as far as the forks of the Porcupine to find out."

When he hesitated, the sheriff asked: "And what was it?"

"Someone had hauled a scoop up there on a sled. They'd dug out the Porcupine and thrown a dam across the Owl."

Echols's back stiffened. "Say that again!"

Frank nodded. Then, with a spare smile that mirrored a trace of his dislike for this man, he drawled: "Funny thing. We'd no sooner seen what they'd done down there than all of a sudden some of that rotten rimrock cut loose and dragged down maybe a thousand tons of the south wall. Dumped it smack across that cut. Now the Porcupine's dammed up solid as though it'd never been there. All that water's coming down the Owl and out across Anchor."

He deeply relished the effect of his bland announcement. Jim Echols stood, open-mouthed, for once struck completely dumb. And in another moment he added with studied casualness: "Part of the dam's still left. Kate thought you might like to come up and look it over, along with the sled tracks down along the Porcupine."

The lawman's face had turned a deep red. "That rock cut loose all by itself, of course."

"Of course, Sheriff."

Frank expected some outburst from the man. Yet it didn't come. Instead, Echols regarded him in an oddly speculative way a long moment, finally saying: "If I live to be a hundred and fifty, I'll never catch onto how Lute Pleasants's mind works. Why would he try and get away with anything as raw as stealin' Anchor's water?"

"He could've been playing the chance of the freeze-up lasting till spring. By then no one could have told why the Owl was running low."

"That I know. But what's eatin' the man? It's a cinch he's rigged it with Crowe to string that fence. Why? What's he after? Does he still think Fred and Kate had his fence cut and tolled Cauble up there the other night so they could kill him?"

Frank only shook his head, giving no answer, whereupon the lawman breathed in a disheartened way: "Can't make head or tail of any of this. Of the way Pleasants is throwin' his weight around. Or," he pointedly added, "of you."

"What about me?"

"That shot the other night." Echols was all at once studying Frank closely, very alertly. "Who knew you'd be on your way across from Summit that night? And even if they did, why would they want to put a bullet into you?"

"When I find out, I'll let you know."

"Maybe there's something you're keepin' back, Rivers. Could be you drifted in here to hunt down some jasper. He could have got wind of it. Is that a good guess?"

"You forgot, Sheriff. I'm only wandering around trying to make the governor's pardon look good."

This barbed reminder of their differences oddly failed to rouse the lawman. Instead, it turned him completely sober, and with a level glance at Frank he observed: "Guess you could say I had that comin'." Then, as though in apology, he added: "A man gets to thinkin' one way so long it's hard for him to change."

Suddenly and without understanding quite how it had come about, Frank was feeling a growing respect for Jim Echols. The man had just now plainly admitted that he might have been mistaken in his judgment of the Peak City affair.

This fact was so unsettling, so unexpected, that Frank for the second time chose not to remind the sheriff further of the rancor that lay between them. He had one more thing on his mind and now spoke of it. "Kate doesn't know it yet, but I'm trying to round up a couple good men to ride for us. Could you put me onto someone?"

"You're that close to being through with the chore?" the lawman asked surprisedly. "Fred spoke of another week or more."

"It may turn out to be another week," Frank answered evasively, the words at complete odds with a plan that had taken shape in his mind on the fast ride down here tonight. "But how about it? Where will I find help?"

Instead of answering, Echols had a question of his own. "Which way will you take the herd out? Over the mountain?"

Once again Frank evaded a direct reply, drawling: "What choice have we got now, with Crowe showing his hand?"

Perhaps the sheriff had suspected that more lay behind what Frank had told him than appeared on the surface. If so, he seemed halfway convinced now that his suspicions were unfounded, for he shook his head, saying: "Findin' men right now is a tall order. This storm spooked folks. Every outfit I know is hirin' heavy and shippin' ahead of time. Hell, they're even loadin' two freights tonight."

Frank had a thought then that made him ask: "What about Bannister and that hired man of his? They're friends of Kate's and Fred's."

The lawman's brows arched in brief speculation. "The old man wouldn't be much help. Besides, someone's got to be on hand up there to hitch the relays for the stages. But he might loan you Will Hepple for a few days."

"Then I'll take the long way around on my way back to the layout."

"If you do, stay away from Crowe."

With a faint smile, Frank said: "Crowe can wait." He half turned from the table. "Well, better be on my way."

155

"Tell Kate I'll try and get up to see Fred in the mornin'."

With a nod, Frank walked on across the room, feeling that Echols had been about to say something more. What that would have been he could only guess. But the fact remained that for all of five minutes Jim Echols had been reasonable, even helpful.

The why of all this confounded him. Wondering about the change in the man, unable to see what lay behind it, he finally put the matter from mind.

The important thing right now was whether or not the buckskin was in shape to carry him up to Summit and across to Anchor tonight. He would take his time, he decided. There was no longer any reason to hurry.

CHAPTER SIXTEEN

T he stars told Frank that it was nearing 1:00 a.m. when he finally glimpsed a light winking palely far above along Anchor's moonlit meadow. The thought that Kate might still be awake, sitting up with Fred, made him gently prod the tired buckskin from its steady walk into a slow jog.

Back there along the Summit road he had found the exact spot below the rim where he had lain in the snow the other night, waiting for the ambusher to ride within range. Looking off toward the timber, he relived the instant the rifle shot had blazed out at him, and in that moment he was positive he could have ridden across there and found the exact spot from which the killer had made his try.

Going on, he made a mental note of getting back there—tomorrow possibly—and looking around up in the timber. A little snow still lay under the pines, and it had been his thought that he might at least pick up the ambusher's tracks. Perhaps they would tell him something.

Just now he rode past bunches of grazing cattle and deer and several of the high-mounded stacks of wild timothy with their circle fences of unpeeled aspen poles. And presently he could make out the big log house's sprawling outline against its backdrop of towering spruce trees and see that the light was shining feebly from the front window of Fred's room in the building's short wing.

At the barn corral he hurried in taking off the saddle. His stride was quick, his tiredness almost forgotten as he walked on up from the harness shed toward the house.

He was coming in on the darkened bunkhouse when old Wade Collins's spare shape moved out of the deep shadows and into the moonlight to intercept him. Collins carried a rifle slacked in the bend of an arm and, joining him, asked querulously: "Where you been? Kate's in a stew."

"Came back by way of Summit," Frank answered. "Will Hepple's coming across in the morning to give us a hand for as long as we need him."

"Good. We can use him."

"How goes it with Fred?"

"Lightfoot gave him something to quiet him down. Damn those murderin' sidewinders." The old man's eyes went narrow-lidded, and in a voice trembling with emotion he added: "Just got back from takin' a swing down around their camp. Frank, between us we could make it hotter'n the hinges for those three devils. Tonight. Right now! They got their tent in a draw, with not even a man on watch. All we need's buckshot. We can catch . . ."

"Not just yet," Frank cut in. Then, because he

sensed the cold fury that was gripping the other, he told him: "We move the herd out first. Then we'll see about squaring things for Fred."

Sighing his disgust, Collins wanted to know: "When'll that be? A week from now, like Fred planned? That's too long to wait."

"It's for Kate to decide, Wade."

"For you, too. That girl's countin' on you. So am I."

Impressed and sobered by such a statement from this ordinarily close-mouthed and undemonstrative old man, Frank said—"We'll see."—and walked on toward the two big spruce trees marking the path leading to the house.

He was halfway up the path when he saw Kate sitting on the top step of the porch at the joining of the cabin's two wings. And as he came on she uncrossed her arms that had been folded over her knees and reached up in an unconscious gesture to run her hands back over her chestnut hair.

She smiled across at him as he halted just short of the bottom step. "Now everything's all right," she said, very softly. "I was afraid something had happened to you."

He told her briefly of his visit to the Bannisters in Summit, of eating a late supper there, and of Will Hepple's coming, then asked: "What did Lightfoot have to say?"

"Fred's going to be all right. The doctor gave him some chloroform before he worked on the arm. He's going to be carrying it in a sling for a few days. He dropped off to sleep an hour ago."

"What about his ribs, his insides?"

"No ribs broken, and nothing else very serious." Hesitating, Kate added: "Fred was lucky. Very lucky. Just think how much worse it could have been for him." She reached over and laid a hand on the step alongside her. "Sit down, Frank. You must be played out."

He came up the steps and eased his high frame down onto the porch's edge beside her, very aware of her nearness and of the beauty of her face in the moonlight. He caught the faintest trace of the scent she wore, and, as it had its heady effect on him, he realized that this girl's every gesture and glance, her way of speaking, even the way she used her hands, had its special meaning for him. Never had he felt so powerfully drawn to a woman, or so awed and humbly pleased at thinking that one should trust and respect him as completely as Kate did.

When he spoke to her, it was in a low voice, for the open side window of Fred's bedroom was less than six feet away. "Had a talk with friend Echols. He took it pretty well." Laughing softly, he went on: "He didn't swallow my tall tale about the slide cutting loose on its own. But he didn't get sore, either. He's coming out in the morning if he can get away."

Kate nodded almost absent-mindedly, her

thoughts obviously having strayed to something else. "What about tomorrow, Frank?"

He shifted around until he could eye her more directly, abruptly deciding to speak his mind. "Why do we wait any longer on moving that beef, Kate? Any reason why we can't push out the best of what we've gathered, then get to work afterward on what's still in the hills?"

She smiled in a way he didn't understand until she said: "You've been reading my mind. I've been wondering the same thing."

A small stir of excitement lifted in him. "Then you're for it?"

"Yes. It's a long drive over that mountain, Frank. The sooner we start, the better."

Very deliberately, he queried: "Why over the mountain?"

He saw her stiffen and stare at him closely. "Because it's our only choice."

"No." His single word was clipped, unarguable.

He began talking then with an urgency in his tone, putting many more words together at one time than was his habit. And he finished by insisting: "It can be done. But now, before it's too late."

A worried frown had gathered on Kate's face. "It would be a risk, a big one. Especially for you, Frank."

"So's the other. A bigger one when you add it all up."

"And if they try and stop us?"

"They won't. I've told you why."

She clasped her arms about her knees and for an interval stared at him as though carefully studying every feature of his lean face. Finally she told him: "It's you I'm thinking about. Something could happen to you."

He smiled, drawling: "Something could happen to 'most anybody, Kate. One of the toughest bruisers I ever knew slipped off a walk up in Peak City one rainy day, hit the back of his head on a plank, and gave up the ghost without ever knowing what happened to him."

"This is different and you know it. If anything goes wrong, it could mean the end of Anchor."

He nodded reluctantly. "So it could. But for a minute there it seemed a good way of squaring things for what they did to Fred."

Quite suddenly Kate's grave look thinned and died away. Perhaps it was what he had said, or even his tone, that caused the abrupt change in her way of looking at this. For now she told him: "I shouldn't be arguing. You're the one who's managing things now. Of course your way's the best."

"I don't have the say in this, Kate. You do."

"All right then." Very positively she added: "We do it your way, Frank. Because I say it's the best way. Now let's go over it again, all of it."

CHAPTER SEVENTEEN

They ate their breakfast in Anchor's kitchen as the new day's first light thinned the blackness over the craggy peaks to the east. By the time it was full light, Frank and Collins were working bunches of cattle down across the upper meadow toward the ranch buildings. In another half hour Will Hepple came up the Summit road, saw them, and rode to join them.

Last night Kate had told Frank of a broad, narrow-necked pocket in the timber at the southeastern end of the meadow, something like a mile and a half below Anchor's headquarters. Lacking enough help to round up the six or seven hundred animals spread out over the meadow, Frank and Collins had decided to work bunches of a hundred or more, cut out the likely ones, then drive them down to hold them in this natural though crude enclosure until they had made up the shipping herd.

Frank's arm was much better this morning, still stiff but having lost its swollen, feverish feel. Surprisingly enough, his less than four hours of sleep had completely refreshed him and he worked steadily and fast, eager to finish this tedious preliminary to the moment Kate and Wade Collins were waiting for and even dreaded, the moving of the shipping herd down to the railroad.

The lush, long vista of the meadow was having a strange effect on Frank this sunny, bright morning. Even though it didn't remotely resemble the land around his homestead, far to the north, he was thinking of the homestead with a yearning he couldn't thrust aside.

These last three days of living on a well-ordered layout, of working the clock around, and of being with people he liked and trusted, had made him see things far differently than at any time since the nightmare of his arrest and trial. It gave him a warm feeling to think that he had found real friends in this out-of-the-way spot, friends who knew of his past and still believed in him.

Quite honestly, and with a degree of genuine surprise, he admitted that the singleness of purpose that had driven him over the past four months was weakening. He had, in fact, completely forgotten it for hours at a time yesterday and the day before. This morning, try as he would, he couldn't manage to summon that same stubborn resolve he had brought with him to Ute Springs.

It still did matter a great deal that the two men responsible for his father's untimely passing were still at large. But just now he was recalling nearly forgotten dreams of the homestead, of what he would one day make of it. And he found himself longing to return to it, to put an end to this futile wandering and to thrust down roots so that he would have a place he could call home, a place like Anchor was for Kate and Fred.

Perhaps the sharing of Fred's and Kate's worries had given him a new perspective on his own. But the fact remained that from this day onward he would never be so unalterably convinced that he must keep on with his hunt and somehow track down the lame carpenter and the man who had sided him on the road below Peak City that night almost five years ago.

Thinking back on all that had happened to him since coming here, he found much that was puzzling, inexplicable. The shot from the rim the other night was most confounding of all because he couldn't tie it in with anything that had happened beforehand. The more he thought about it, the more incongruous it became that anyone in this country would have knowingly picked him as a target. It even seemed quite likely that the ambusher had mistaken him for someone else.

For the past quarter hour he had been working the meadow's edge. And just now Wade Collins rode across and hailed him to interrupt his futile speculation. The old man's eyes were bloodshot from an almost sleepless night and his tone was barbed as he nodded toward the ranch buildings below, saying: "Jim Echols rode in ten minutes ago. What's Kate going to tell him about what we're doing?"

"Probably the truth. We're cutting the shipping herd." Frank looked below, shortly saying: "Maybe I ought to get down there and see what he has to say. Can you spare me?"

Collins at once nodded. "Sure. Will and me can manage. The main thing is to get Echols out of here."

Frank swung the buckskin away and started down across the meadow at an easy lope. He was still something like a quarter mile short of the ranch buildings when he saw two riders, Kate and Jim Echols, round the spur of spruce concealing the house and come toward him. He pulled in on the buckskin and went on at a walk to meet them.

As he joined them, Jim Echols surprisingly was cordial as he announced: "Kate's taking me up for a look at that dam. Want to come along?"

"Better not. Too much to do here." Frank turned the buckskin and fell in alongside them, next to Kate. "How's Fred doing?"

"He's turned ornery." Kate gave him a smile that let him know she was glad to be with him. "He's up and dressed and sitting in a chair."

"And talkin' about workin' tomorrow," the lawman added.

Frank grinned broadly, somehow pleased at hearing this last. "You Bonds are tough as Cheyennes. Let him do what he wants."

"But that arm's useless," Kate protested

166

worriedly. "If he does try and ride, he's liable to hurt himself."

"Then keep him hog-tied," Echols suggested.

The remark didn't seem to satisfy Kate, and they rode on back up the meadow without speaking for a good two minutes, until Frank finally said: "Here's where I leave you." He nodded toward Collins and Hepple, who were some three hundred yards away, steadily pushing a bunch of white-faces southward.

Echols reined in, looked at Frank. "When we get back, I'm goin' across to Summit to try and throw a scare into Crowe. I'll lay you a dollar to a dime he doesn't know anything about what they did to Fred."

"Probably not." Frank had a thought then that made him ask: "Mind if I side you part of the way?"

They had reined in, their horses at a stand, and now Echols's expression turned quizzical. "Sure, come along. But why?"

"I thought I might look over the spot where that shot came from the other night."

The lawman's glance sharpened with quick interest. "Now that's a good notion. We'll make short work of this other." He led the way on then, Kate lifting a hand to Frank as she left him.

It was nearly two hours before they rode back down from the head of the meadow, by which time Frank, Collins, and Will Hepple were pushing the animals they had cut from the main herd on past the ranch buildings. Frank had half an hour ago ridden in to see Fred, had found him almost cheerful, and also very inquisitive about plans for getting the shipping herd out. Frank answered his questions evasively, knowing that, if he told him of what he and Kate had talked about last night, there would be no keeping him in the house for the rest of the day.

Jim Echols was much impressed, even awed, by what he had seen up along the rim above the Porcupine, though Frank didn't discover that until some ten minutes after they left Kate and, following the twin tracks of the Summit road, reached the roaring creek at a spot where they had to wade a long stretch that was flooded from the stream's overflow.

Looking out across the acre or more of ground covered by the water, Echols soberly said: "Pleasants'll play hell ever bustin' that slide clear. It must've been a sight when it cut loose."

"So it was."

The lawman glanced around, dryly drawling: "It'd take someone like you to make Pleasants eat this kind of crow. What'll Kate and Fred do with all this water?"

"Maybe the same as Pleasants planned . . . dig ditches and double their hay crop."

"Wish Amy and John could have lived to see it." There was an undiluted quality of wistfulness in

Echols's tone. "That's all John ever wanted beyond what he had. More water, so he could grow enough feed to carry him over the winters."

"Well, Anchor's got it now."

"And Pleasants hasn't." The sheriff laughed softly and apparently in genuine merriment. "Wonder how long it'll take him to come to me and raise a howl?"

"If he does, take him up there and show him what's left of his dam."

"I'll do that and don't think I won't." Seriously the sheriff went on: "Things have switched around some. He'll have some water from a few springs that feed the Porcupine above his place. But he'll never be able to run those feeders now. Ten to one he'll have to trim down his herd from lack of grass."

As they went on, Frank was finding it hard to understand the change in Jim Echols. The man had shed the last trace of that caustic, truculent manner that had been so typical of him even as late as their talk at the hotel last night. Today he seemed genuinely friendly, almost easy-going.

In ten more minutes Frank was suggesting that they begin a circle to the south that would take them onto Crowe's range well below the fence camp and the point where the road crossed from Anchor.

"You're duckin' those three hardcases?" the lawman wanted to know. "Why?"

"One thing at a time."

This somewhat cryptic answer prompted Echols to study Frank over a deliberate interval, which ended by his shrewdly commenting: "I'd give a lot to know what's goin' on in that think tank of yours. But if you say so, we don't let 'em see us."

Frank right then had to hold in check the fool-hardy urge to tell him that he wanted the three Beavertail men to believe that the beating they had given Fred had disheartened everyone at Anchor. Only by remembering that Echols was not only a friend of Kate's and Fred's, but also a peace officer, was he able to put down the rash impulse.

It took them another twenty minutes to ride the circle, meet the road again, and finally reach the open stretch footing the rim that Frank remembered so well. After he had pointed out the spot where he had seen the rifle's flash, Echols seemed to want to take charge.

And oddly enough, he also seemed to want to put last things first. For after asking several questions and listening closely to Frank's answers, he suggested: "First off, let's find the place where you took out after this jasper. Up there in the trees."

Puzzled, Frank nonetheless led the way across from the road to the margin of the pines, shortly coming onto the line of the buckskin's tracks striking upward across the shaded, unmelted snow.

The lawman got down to look at the tracks, then

followed them all the way to the bare crest of the rim. There, he turned right and finally sloped down the far side along the line the ambusher had taken in making his getaway. Down in the shelter of the pines he came across more tracks and once again swung aground, kneeling to examine them.

When he straightened, he looked up at the tall man who had been observing all this with such bridled impatience. "Different," he said.

Frank didn't catch his meaning. "Different from what?"

"From that sign down below."

Suddenly Frank understood. Jim Echols had come up here purposely to prove to himself that more than one rider, someone other than Frank, had been on the rim that night.

Frank's instant reaction was one of high indignation over the man's unbreakable mistrust of him. For a moment he groped for something to say, for some scalding, biting remark that would really sting the sheriff. But then all at once it didn't matter, and, when he spoke, his tone was only faintly disdainful.

"Well, now you've seen it."

Echols looked across at him soberly to say, with surprising candor: "Give a man time, will you, Rivers? After all, Bill Echols is still in that wheel chair."

"And I'm still hunting the men that put him there."

The sheriff's head tilted in a slow nod. "I'm beginnin' to think maybe you are. For the first time."

This unlooked-for admission at another time would have meant a lot to Frank. Now it didn't. All that mattered at the moment was to finish what he had come for, and to part company with Echols as soon as possible. "Do we go back down there now and have a look at where he was when he threw his shot?"

"We do."

It took them nearly twenty minutes, ten to find the tracks of the ambusher's horse close to the spot where Frank thought he had seen the rifle's flash, another ten of searching the ground nearby, which was at the very margin of the pines and now only lightly covered with melting snow.

Jim Echols was the one who made the find. Caught in the thorny and interlaced stems of a wild rose bush he spotted a dull brass shell case and called Frank across to see where it had wedged itself before he leaned down to retrieve it.

Holding it in his palm and looking at it, he remarked: "You said it sounded like a heavy rifle. Here, take a look."

He tossed the hollow brass cylinder across to Frank. The shell appeared familiar at first glance, seeming to be exactly like the .44-40s Frank used in his Winchester. But then Frank noticed the shallow shoulder a third of the way down from the neck of the shell. He didn't have to inspect the numbers stamped on its bottom to say positively: "Forty-Five-Seventy-Five." He eyed the lawman speculatively. "Can't be too many of these around, can there?"

"No. Amos Bent ought to be able to help us. He's the man in town that fixes guns."

"Then this may prove something?"

"It may," was all Echols would say.

"It would if you could find another one like it, wouldn't it?" Frank drawled.

As the sheriff frowned in puzzlement, Frank added: "Another one up where Cauble was killed."

Jim Echols's eyes came wider open. He let his breath go in a soft whistle. "Why didn't I think of that? Can you take me up there? Now?"

Frank was at first tempted to make the ride. But when he realized that they could easily spend the rest of the day finding the place where he had camped above Pleasants's fence and searching the slope above it—when he remembered what he and Kate had planned for this evening—he shook his head.

"Can't do it now. Too much going on back at the layout."

"Tomorrow then? Early?"

Frank nodded. "Tomorrow."

CHAPTER EIGHTEEN

Fred Bond was completely winded by the time he got the saddle on the claybank and pulled himself astride the animal. He sat with head hanging for all of a minute until the pounding of his heart and the aching of his shoulder and side had eased off.

Then, very gingerly, he lifted reins and took the claybank away from the corral at a walk, heading down across the meadow in the gathering darkness, guided by the pinpoint winking of a fire from far below.

That blaze marked the near end of the pocket into which he had all afternoon watched Collins, Will Hepple, and Kate—and finally Frank—drive small bunches of steers and heifers that were to make up the shipping herd. And as he let the claybank hurry its stride to a jog, finding his aching body could stand the jolting of the saddle, he was smiling crookedly at recalling the seeming innocence with which Kate had come up to the house an hour ago, fixing him his supper, and then given him the excuse of having to ride back down the meadow again to see when the men, who were working late, planned to eat.

Presently he was close enough to make out their shapes around the fire, Frank Rivers's rangy outline towering over the others. He laughed aloud then, thinking of the surprise he had in store for them.

Frank was the first to hear him coming, and swung away, stepping into the shadows as he rode into the circle of firelight. He reined in and sat, grinning down at Kate, who stared at him as though not believing what her eyes were showing her.

"Thought you were all going to eat at the house," he said, nodding down to the tin plates, the Dutch oven, and the cups sitting near the blaze.

The next moment Frank reappeared and strode over alongside the claybank, asking sharply: "What's this, Fred?"

"Right on time, aren't I?" Fred peered down at the tall man with that grin still patterning his swollen and scarred face. He lifted his bad arm in its sling. "I'm all right, so don't start reading me the gospel, Frank. I was awake last night while you and Kate were gabbing out there on the porch. So try to get rid of me."

Kate managed to find her voice now and said hollowly: "Fred, you've lost your mind. Get back . . ."

"Save your breath, girl. I'm coming with you."

Kate gave Frank a look that begged him to help her talk Fred out of this insane notion. Yet there had been a quality of iron in Fred's tone that wasn't to be argued, and now Frank only shook his head sparely and turned away, not wanting to interfere.

The argument began in earnest then, Collins heatedly joining Kate to persuade Fred he was playing the fool. But all Fred did was sit there, leaning on his good arm and shaking his head, until finally he told them: "Give up, will you? I've come this far and I'm in better shape than when I started. So I tag along."

"Frank, can't you do something about this?" Kate was really angry now, seeming to resent Frank's holding himself aloof from the argument.

Realizing this, Frank was nonetheless able to put himself in Fred's place and halfway feel a measure of the bitterness and the longing for revenge he knew must be gripping the man. Fred deserved the chance he was asking for tonight.

"No, Kate," Frank at length told her. "After last night he can do anything he wants. It's up to him."

"But think of . . ."

"It's no go, Sis. I'm in on this. More than that, I'm siding Frank."

The words came as a shock to Frank, whose head jerked around so that he could meet the man's glance. "No you don't, friend. That part I do on my own."

"Think again," Fred came back at him. "You need help and you know it." He reached down and slapped the stock of the rifle he had tied to his saddle. "You do the leg work, I furnish the fire-works."

Miserably Kate put in: "Let's give the whole thing up. Will can go home. We'll wait till another day."

"No." Frank, oddly enough, was suddenly beginning to believe that Fred just might mean the difference between things working smoothly tonight or possibly not at all, short-handed as they were. And he looked at Kate to say seriously: "His being along could make my end of it twice as easy. But there's one thing that's got to be understood." He glanced up at Fred once again, a flintiness in his blue eyes as he drawled: "We're not collecting any scalps tonight."

Fred nodded readily enough. "No scalps. But someone's going to be feeling a hell of a sight older when this is finished. And it won't be you and me."

That was the end of it. Even Kate didn't argue now, Frank's words having made her resignedly accept the risk Fred was running in going with them. Perhaps she even began to understand this in the same way Frank did, for she shortly brought a cup of coffee across and handed it up to her brother, giving him a smile, saying: "You always were a brat. But a nice one."

Ten minutes later the work started for everyone but Fred, who sat his horse watching the bawling heifers and steers being pushed out from the holding ground onto the meadow. Full darkness was on them now, yet the starlight was bright enough to let them see individual animals at some distance as the herd strung out and swung south across the lower end of the meadow.

There were upward of two hundred head in the herd. Collins and Frank worked the drag, Will Hepple and Kate rode the swings, Fred the point. For something like forty minutes they drove steadily southward, reaching the end of the meadow and then moving along behind a series of ridges showing their shadowed outlines to the west, until finally Frank swung over to Collins and said briefly—"Here's where I leave you."—and rode on ahead in the darkness.

At the head of the strung-out line of animals he angled over until he made out Fred's shape. "Let's be at it!" he called, and they pulled on ahead, striking west of the line they had been following.

Presently Fred pulled close alongside Frank. "Get me planted up there above the tent and I won't budge."

"You're going to have to move around some." Frank went on talking, explaining, finally asking: "How gun-shy is that claybank?"

"He isn't. Which is why I picked him."

"Good. Be sure you tie him where you can get to him fast if you have to."

They rode steadily on for the better part of

another quarter hour, until abruptly Frank pulled in and pointed ahead, saying tersely: "There's the line. Which way now?"

"Right a little."

They crossed the line dividing Anchor from Crowe's land, the mounds of dirt around several post holes showing plainly in the starlight. And shortly Frank was seeing the glow of a fire's light reflected against a thick stand of aspen climbing the far side of a draw five or six hundred yards ahead. This was Crowe's fence camp.

He drew rein, let Fred come even with him, then softly said: "Pick your spot, get set, and give me plenty of time. I'll start things off unless you have to first."

"Which I won't. No reason for 'em to be moving about."

Frank nodded. "How you feeling?"

"Never better. Never."

"Watch that shoulder. And remember to move around. I don't want to be packing you home across that hull."

"Nor me you."

Frank drew on ahead now, beginning a wide circle that in ten more minutes took him to the top of a low ridge at a point a hundred yards below the tent and rope corral Beavertail's crew had put in sometime yesterday.

He tied the buckskin on the far slope of the ridge, drew the Winchester from its scabbard, then began working his way down through the trees on the slope below the camp. Once when he paused and looked below, he could plainly make out figures squatting or standing near the fire. And his pulse quickened as he counted four men instead of three and plainly recognized one of these as being Lute Pleasants.

This was more than he'd hoped for, certainly more than Fred had, either, and a heady excitement was building in him as he walked carefully on. He had tied his spurs to his saddle and he moved soundlessly except for the occasional faint metallic jingling of the shells cramming both pockets of his pants.

In two more minutes he had forgotten the men at the fire above the tent and was carefully scanning the shadows ahead where seven horses were feeding in the improvised corral made of ropes stretched between the trees.

Once he reached the bottom of the draw, he came straight in on the animals, knowing that to walk openly up to them was less liable to spook them than if he tried to approach too carefully. He was pulling a big clasp knife from his pocket the moment a gelding, seeing him, lifted its head and whickered, alerting the others.

They stood quietly watching him as he sauntered in on the ropes. He made three quick slashes with the knife, cutting the ropes. Then, moving on around and toward the tent, he reached the upper side of the corral, the animals turning slowly, warily, still eyeing him.

He took off his hat now and all at once lifted it over his head and violently waved it.

The nearest horse reared, turned, and bolted. The others panicked instantly, whirling and following the first, their hoofs drumming solidly against the damp earth as they ran out through the gap in the ropes.

Suddenly from close behind him came a shout: "Who's that?"

Instinctively, without looking around, he lunged for the trunk of the nearest pine. That same instant the hard explosion of a gun behind him sent its deafening thunder out across the draw.

CHAPTER NINETEEN

Two minutes ago, standing at the fire in front of the tent at the fence camp, Lute Pleasants had told Red, Ben, and Harry: "I'd better be getting back to the layout. You're to just go ahead like you have been, working the fence. But stay together. And if anyone from Anchor shows up, don't take any guff. If it's Rivers, give him a working over like you did Bond." He intercepted the skeptical glance Ben Galt gave Red Majors, and bridled: "Hell, he's only one man, isn't he?"

No one spoke up in answer to his barbed question, and on this truculent note he turned and left them, going on past the tent and down through the trees toward the corral.

His thoughts were still disdainfully centered on the scene back there, on the doubt he had seen in the eyes of all three of his crewmen at his suggestion of their standing up to Rivers. For that reason he wasn't wholly prepared for what he encountered as he came down to the corral.

He had a fleeting glimpse of what he took to be a man's vague outline standing between two trees. One instant he thought he saw the figure with arm upraised, waving something. The next he caught the muffled pound of the horses, bolting away down the draw.

"Who's that?" he bawled stridently, snatching his gun from his holster.

He tried to lay his sights on that indistinct figure close ahead, yet whoever it was moved sharply aside at the precise moment the .45 pounded against his wrist.

Pleasants bellowed an oath and tried to line his weapon once more. But the figure had disappeared somewhere off to his left. From up the slope there sounded the sudden racket of a man running through brush, and Pleasants swung the .45 around and emptied it at the sound.

His trembling hands were shucking fresh shells from his belt when all at once a rifle shot cracked down into the draw from high along the ridge above the tent. At the fire Ben Galt shouted lustily, either in pain or fear, the sound of his voice cut short by a second explosion from the rifle off there.

Just then from the slope above Pleasants a second rifle opened up deliberately, bullet after bullet smashing down through the nearby trees. One whining ricochet from the trunk of a tree close at hand suddenly drew Pleasants's muscles tight. He turned and ran as hard as he could back up the draw toward the tent.

Ahead of him a shower of sparks flew into the air as a bullet from one of the rifles smashed into a glowing log. Then, as Pleasants swung sharply to his left toward the shelter of a windfall, the metallic clang of a bullet smashing Red Majors's Dutch oven rode down the draw.

Pleasants threw himself behind the two-foot-thick trunk of the windfall. He was breathing hard, cursing with every breath, realizing now that whoever had been down at the corral had stampeded the horses, that he and his crew were afoot.

Longing for a target, he peered up the opposite slope. And shortly, as the rifles kept up their deliberate, slow-timed fire, he did spot the flash of one of them, the closest. But as he came to his knees and brought up the Colt, he abruptly checked himself, sanity finally having its way with him.

If he fired at the flash of that rifle, he would give away his own position. Every muscle in him went rigid at the thought of the rifle searching him out if he missed the man firing it. And common sense told him that his target was too distant for a sure hit.

So he crouched there, wincing at each shot that lanced down from the ridge into the camp. He heard a bullet smash into the water bucket and send it rolling in toward the tent. He heard the lantern on the front pole of the tent clang and fall to the ground. And afterward flames leaped up, outlining the tent until its canvas caught and burned, shedding a blaze of strong light over this lower reach of the draw.

Up ahead he could see Harry hugging the thick

trunk of a pine. Ben and Red were out of sight, and the thought that their rifles were in the burning tent, that not one of the three had had the foresight or the guts to go after a Winchester, infuriated him until he could feel his pulse pounding at his temples.

Exactly how long it was before the two rifles on the ridge went silent, Pleasants didn't know. But suddenly he was aware that the two men up there had stopped shooting.

Warily, his quick glance searching the ridge, he came up out of his crouch and walked slowly up toward the smoldering ruin of the tent. From off to his left Ben Galt called very softly: "That you, boss?"

"Who the hell else would it be?"

Galt's thick bulk materialized out of the blackness. "You hear that?" he asked.

"What?"

"Cattle bawlin'. Listen."

Pleasants halted. Then he caught it. Out of the distance, from very far to the south, he could hear it, the bawling of cattle.

"Well, guess we was a little late on that fence," Galt said solemnly, ruefully. "There goes Anchor, chousin' their beef for the pass road. Come noon tomorrow and they'll be in sight of the Springs."

CHAPTER TWENTY

This past hour and a half had seemed a near eternity to Kate. In the beginning it hadn't been so bad, for with only the help of Will Hepple and Wade Collins, ranging the flanks of the herd, she had her hands full to keep the straggling, bawling animals in the drag moving steadily on along the Summit road.

But then suddenly the sounds of the guns had rolled in out of the westward distance, and her imagination had begun to run riot. She reined in and listened, noticing that Will and Wade also momentarily forgot their work.

When the rifles' slow-spaced racket kept on for minute after minute, she found it unbearable not knowing what was going on across there. And a feeling of utter helplessness gripped her as she began riding once more, determined not to pay the sound of the guns the slightest attention.

For upward of the next quarter hour she had ridden so hard and fast that her horse began playing out. Finally, reining him in to a walk, she let the herd draw on ahead. And all at once she had become aware of those far-away shots having died out.

That had been forty minutes ago. And now, as each minute dragged by without Fred or Frank appearing, her worry heightened until she scarcely knew what she was doing.

The herd was straggling badly. Will and Wade seeming unable to keep the swing animals moving so as to push the lead ones on at any speed at all. She did what she could to keep the drag bunched and on the move. But minute by minute the gait of the heifers and steers dropped to a slower walk until finally she knew that she and Wade and Will could no longer manage this chore without help.

It was perhaps half a minute after this disheartening realization came to her that a series of whooping shouts sounded in across the night from off beyond the west flank of the herd. That voice was unmistakably Fred's, and, as she heard Will and Wade join him in a series of high-pitched shouts so typical of men working cattle, a wave of delight and relief gripped her. She threw her spurs into her horse's flanks and rode recklessly in among the drag animals then, whipping them with rein ends to stir them out of their ambling.

A faint uneasiness held her as she wondered about Frank, wondered why he hadn't called out along with Fred. But she tried not to think of that as she steadily worked back and forth across the drag, feeling the herd falter at first, then stir from its lethargy as though the shouting had awakened it. And in another minute her horse was having to move at a brisk jog to keep up with even the laggards.

All at once she made out a rider's shape drifting back toward her from up ahead and to her right. And in another moment Fred was calling: "Wake up, Sis! We're back."

He had said—"We're back."—which could only mean that Frank was with him. Kate reached out and laid a hand on his good arm as he swung in abreast her. And her voice was none too steady as she breathed: "You're all right?"

"Never better." He laughed boisterously. "Guess what. Lute was there."

"No!"

"Damned if Frank didn't sneak down there right under their noses and turn their nags loose. He ran smack into Lute. The devil had a clear try at him and missed. That Frank now, there's a man."

"He wasn't hurt?"

"Not a scratch, either of us. We shot at everything in sight. Frank even got the lantern and set their tent afire. They didn't throw so much as one chunk of lead at us."

Kate was feeling the aftereffects of this long interval of suspense and worry, and now she laughed delightedly, asking: "Then we've got an hour or two before they can catch up with us?"

"An hour or two? We've got a week if we want it. Frank made me tag along while he choused their jugheads about three miles off toward Beavertail. All those birds'll do tonight will be to wear out the soles of their boots. We're in the clear."

"Thanks to Frank," Kate said very softly.

"Amen." Fred's tone was quite solemn as he asked: "How can we ever make it up to him, Sis?"

"I don't know, Fred."

"Couldn't he stick around after this is finished? Couldn't we persuade him to . . . ?" He shrugged, at a loss for words. Then shortly he added: "I keep forgetting. He's got this other on his mind. Chances are we'll see him driftin' on in another day or two."

"We will?"

Kate's voice sounded small, lost. Throughout this long and anxious day she hadn't given a thought to anything beyond the moment when, with luck, Anchor's herd would be safely across Crowe's range and on the pass road, headed for the low country and Ute Springs.

Now, with Fred's unwelcome reminder coming so unexpectedly, this cool and starry night lost its heady exhilaration as an emotion akin to despair settled slowly through her.

Twenty minutes of working with Will Hepple and Wade Collins satisfied Frank that the herd was no longer lagging. Fred had some time ago disappeared back toward the drag to look for Kate, and now, knowing that Collins and Hepple could spare him, Frank drew aside and pulled the buckskin to a stand, watching the long file of bawling cattle move on past as he packed and lighted his pipe.

The first faint glow of the late-rising moon sharply etched the peaks in the upward distance, and Frank, some of the feeling of urgency having left him, welcomed the thought that in another half hour they would be able to see more of what they were doing. Luck had been with them, the night having hid their moving the herd onto and across Crowe's range. Now, when it counted the most, they would presently have enough light to let them work the herd more easily and push on faster.

He had been sitting there for not quite two minutes, right leg crooked around the horn of the saddle and left boot hanging free of stirrup, when Fred loped up out of the blackness, saw him, and swung over to join him.

Fred was breathing hard, and it was obvious that he was excited even before he announced: "Got me an idea just now, Frank."

"So have I. You're to head straight on home, crawl into that bed, and sleep till noon tomorrow."

"And miss all this? Think again. I'm seeing this beef all the way to the pens down at the Springs even if I have to crawl the last ten miles."

On the ride across here from the fence camp, Frank had several times noticed that Fred's swollen face was tight with pain. And more than once he had seen him sitting canted around in the saddle, favoring his hurt side. Thinking of that, he dryly remarked: "You're not proving much, half killing yourself. Give it up. The four of us can manage."

"What I've got in mind'll take just the two of us," Fred countered mysteriously. "And we've got to ride only three miles to do it."

When Frank's lean face took on a puzzled frown, Fred added: "You and me are going to pay Phil Crowe a nice neighborly visit."

"Now? In the middle of the night?"

"Why not? He never shuts down that whiskey parlor before midnight. And it can't be much after ten yet unless the stars are lying."

Frank lowered his leg and thrust boots in stirrups, then reached over to knock the dottle from his pipe, asking: "What good will it do you to rub it in on Crowe?"

"The same good it did us both to bust that camp apart back there. Now you coming with me or do I go at it alone?"

Frank sighed resignedly, in no way relishing the prospect of letting Fred take on still another risk tonight. The fact of the man's even being here seemed a minor miracle in itself when he thought back upon last night and that first glimpse he'd had of him, lying in the buckboard there alongside the corral at Anchor.

Yet here he was, his spirits still high, some indomitable drive sustaining him. Frank's reasoning right then became much the same as it had been back at the fire on the meadow two hours ago when Fred laid down the ultimatum that he was riding tonight. After all, this was the night Fred Bond had labored and lived for these many trying weeks. He deserved whatever he could get out of it to balance the disheartening presence of Lute Pleasants's fence and the beating he had taken little more than twenty-four hours ago.

So, dubious though he was over any good coming out of what Fred was suggesting, Frank nonetheless shrugged his concern aside, drawling: "I guess you're writing your own ticket. So, if you say we see Crowe, we see him."

"That's more like it. Let's be at it."

Frank was disappointed in one thing, something he'd been looking forward to for the past half hour. "What about Kate?"

"What about her? She's stuck back there on the drag. So are Will and Wade stuck if they should get to wondering where we've gone. Besides, we'll be back in something like an hour."

With a hesitant nod, Frank reined aside and led the way up along the strung-out line of cattle. In several minutes he thought he saw Collins working the near swing. Then presently they passed the point of the herd, angled over, and followed the rutted road.

In less than another mile they passed Crowe's line camp and from there on the flanking ridges closed in on the track, which meant that when the herd reached this stretch it would be easier to keep it lined out and moving.

Summit, when they reached the pass road and climbed it, appeared as it had to Frank the other night, either deserted or asleep, with not a light showing against the blackness until they made the bend in the street. Then, as Fred announced— "Here we are."—and swung left to the tie rail in front of a single-story building, Frank did see feeble lamplight glowing behind one large and grimy window.

"How'll I know this Crowe?" he asked as he tied the buckskin.

"He'll be wearing a derby, a gray one. Never've seen him without it. They claim he sleeps in it." Fred joined him on the walk, asking: "Mind if I do the talking?"

At Frank's quick shake of the head, he went on: "You back me up, if there's anyone else around. Only I want to rub it in on Crowe all by myself."

"Go ahead. Only don't forget to try and tie Pleasants in with Crowe's new fence."

They found only five men in the Pat Hand's stale-aired and poorly lit room. Four of these sat in a smoke-fogged wash of lamplight, playing a hand of draw poker at a table halfway the length of the bar. The fifth, wearing a gray derby, stood leaning against the adjoining table, watching the play.

Phil Crowe glanced up incuriously at the sound of the door opening. The light was bad up there and he couldn't see who this was, though out of habit he moved across and in behind his bar, his narrow face set in its habitual impassivity. Only when he reached up and turned up the wick of the lamp over the bar did he discover who his new customers were.

His face went slack. He looked first at Fred, who came down along the counter now to stand opposite him, then at Frank, who had halted at the front end of the bar. He didn't say anything, neither did Fred nor Frank.

Finally Fred's half smile and the strained silence wore at Crowe's nerves until he abruptly came out with: "Echols stopped by this afternoon and told me all about it, Bond. I swear to God I had nothing to do with that trouble you ran into last night."

Fred nodded sagely, his expression turning mock-sober. "Wonder who did?"

The saloon man only shrugged and shook his head, not replying.

"Pleasants?"

Crowe's look turned wary. "Them three work for me now. They just up and did it on their own."

"And they work for you." Once again Fred nodded. He eyed a gallon jug sitting on the counter close by, and then, as though deciding he would have a drink, he reached out and uncorked it. Crowe, seeing this, turned to the back shelves and reached for a glass.

By the time he faced the bar again Fred had tipped the jug on its side. It gurgled and began spilling its contents out across the sticky bar top. Crowe opened his mouth to protest, closed it again without speaking, suddenly sensing that he was in for trouble.

The jug was half full and Fred deliberately emptied it, seeming fascinated in watching the whiskey puddle the boards, then spill onto the floor.

The men at the poker layout, having glanced up when Crowe first spoke, watched all this with a scowling, truculent attention until finally one of them, a thick-set individual with close-cropped chin whiskers, laid down his cards and came up out of his chair, calling: "Need any help, Phil?"

Before Crowe could answer, Frank Rivers's soft drawl struck across at him: "Sit down."

The man swung part way around to face this tall stranger. His eyes brightened with malice and for a moment his arms bent slightly, as though he was thinking of the gun he wore butt-foremost high at the left side of his waist.

But something in Frank's lazy stance, in the way he wore his .44 thonged low on his thigh, and in the fact that he hadn't bothered to straighten or even move his elbow from the counter, carried its unmistakable warning.

And when Frank repeated himself just as softly as he had spoken the first time—"Sit down."—the other gripped the arms of his caboose-chair and grudgingly lowered his bulk back down into it.

Fred, having seen all this, now set the empty jug upright, looking at Crowe once more to say: "You and Pleasants are a bit late with your fence. We're driving our beef across your place tonight. The herd'll be on the road below here in another hour."

The saloon man's Adam's apple bobbed and he swallowed with apparent difficulty. When he didn't say anything, Fred went on: "We stranded your crew afoot tonight. Pleasants, too. He was there. Tomorrow, when they've hoofed it after their nags, maybe you better have Pleasants tell 'em to fill in those post holes. Because you're not stringin' that fence."

"The hell you say. No Bond ever told me what to do."

"This Bond's telling you."

Fred's mild-spoken words had barely been uttered when he reached for the jug again. Only this time he picked it up by its handle, drew it back over his shoulder, and suddenly hurled it straight at the center of the long fly-specked mirror that ran the ten-foot length of the backbar shelves.

The crash of the jug smashing the heavy glass sent a tremor along the counter and drowned out Crowe's hoarse and angry cry. The mirror shattered into hundreds of fragments that came jangling down over the shelves and onto the floor, knocking over a few glasses and bottles.

Crowe, his look furious, stooped quickly and was reaching in under the bar when Frank Rivers called sharply: "No you don't!"

His voice seemed to paralyze the saloon owner. Very slowly, very carefully Crowe straightened and resignedly laid his empty hands palms down on his whiskey-puddled bar.

Somehow he managed to find the voice to breathe: "That'll cost you a hundred dollars, Bond."

"Only a hundred?" Fred's swollen face took on a wry grin. He looked down at his bad arm in its sling, lifting his elbow from his side, asking: "Wonder what this bum arm ought to cost *you?*"

When Crowe chose not to answer, Fred unexpectedly moved on back and around the end of the bar. The saloon man turned slowly to watch Fred, his eyes going narrow-lidded as he waited to see what this meant. Fred gave him only a brief moment to wonder. For suddenly with a swing of his good arm he swept a triple tier of glasses from the bottom backbar shelf. The jangle of the breaking glass had barely died away before he swung his arm again, this time emptying the top shelf of two dozen full bottles and stoneware jugs.

A hush lay over the room following the crashing pound of the bottles breaking against the floor planks. Crowe, surveying the ruin about him, appeared stunned, bewildered. The men at the poker layout sat, rigid and unmoving, plainly awed by the violence they had witnessed.

Frank Rivers chose this moment to say: "Let's get back to Pleasants. What did he do, pay you to put in that fence, Crowe?"

The saloon man spun around to face him, snarling: "Be damned to you both! That fence goes in. I'll string it if it takes my last . . ."

His words broke off as he saw Frank move in behind the bar's front end, as he watched the tall man lean back against the shelves at the far end of the empty mirror frame and lift a boot high and place it against the inner edge of the counter. Then, as Frank all at once pushed against the bar, tilting it outward, Crowe shouted: "Don't! By God, I'll . . . !"

The long bar creaked, tipped precariously, overbalanced, and fell outward with a thundering crash that set the lamps to swaying, which brought a back corner of the ceiling showering down in a smother of plaster dust. Kegs that had sat on the shelf under the bar fell on their sides, two buckets of water clanked and spilled their contents across the floor. Three of the men at the table pushed back their chairs, half rose, then sat slowly down again.

And Crowe, driven beyond the point of reason at seeing the ruin of his bar, suddenly lunged for the shotgun he had reached for a minute ago.

Fred saw that, moved in and hit him behind the ear with a swing that had all the drive of his aching body behind it. The saloon man, already stooping over, fell out across his capsized bar and lay groaning, reaching feebly for the shotgun that Fred snatched from under his hand.

Lining the shotgun at the men at the table, Fred swung a boot and ungently prodded Crowe in the ribs. "On your feet!"

Crowe hung his head and awkwardly shoved himself back until he was resting on his knees. Fred poked him in the ribs with the shotgun's twin barrels. "All right, let's have it. How much did Pleasants pay you to string that fence?"

The saloon owner looked up at him, eyes dull with pain and outrage. When he didn't say anything, Frank drawled: "Suppose we finish taking the place apart, Fred."

Crowe called hoarsely—"No!"—and found the strength to stagger erect now. All the starch had gone out of him and he asked miserably: "What is it you want to know?"

"How much did Pleasants pay for the fence?"

Shaking his head to clear his befuddled senses, Crowe peered around at Frank to answer acidly: "Not one damned dollar. He rigged it so I didn't have a chance to turn him down. Said he knew where I'd buried some Anchor hides, which was a lie."

"How long ago was this?" Frank wanted to know.

"The other night? Three, four nights ago?"

All at once Frank came hard alert. "Which night?"

The saloon man at first only shook his head. But then his glance sharpened, and he said: "The night it froze and blew so hard. You ought to remember. You was up here and turned around and rode back down again."

"Pleasants was with you that night?" Frank's tone was roughened by an excitement he was finding it hard to hold in check. "What time did he leave?"

"Right after we saw you go past on your way back down." Crowe sighed wearily, saying: "Now will the two of you clear the hell out and leave me be?"

Frank looked at Fred, who broke the shotgun, took out the shells, and tossed the weapon out across the room so that it hit a chair, knocking it over. Fred stepped on past Crowe, then, drawling: "Remember, fill in those post holes."

Crowe was too humbled to think of a retort as Frank and Fred walked on up to the door. Fred halted there to face around and say: "The man that shows his head outside this door over the next minute is liable to get his hair parted where it'll hurt."

He backed out onto the street, following Frank, and slammed the door.

Neither Crowe nor any of the men at the table so much as stirred until after the hoof pound of a pair of horses had faded out of hearing down the empty street.

CHAPTER TWENTY-ONE

S hortly after midnight Phil Crowe locked the doors of the Pat Hand and, carrying a lantern, crossed the alley, and disappeared inside his small stable. Some minutes later he rode a roan horse down the alley that was now palely lit by the waning moon, which hung above the notch of the pass high to the east.

Below town, Crowe turned into the side road leading to his line camp and Anchor. Once through the notch that hemmed in the track for the first quarter mile, he angled off to the west through the hills and rode for ten minutes before turning north again and following the general direction of the road, thus wisely taking the precaution that he shouldn't again tonight run afoul of anyone from Anchor.

A short time later he plainly heard the bawling of cattle out of the upcountry distance, the sound serving to sour his disposition to such a point that he raged volubly and acidly for a considerable interval.

It took him the better part of another hour to sight the fire of his fence camp, and a figure pacing slowly before it. He knew at once that this was Lute Pleasants, and he found a certain grim pleasure in the way the man, on hearing the roan's approach, hurried back into the shadows beyond the blaze.

"It's me, Crowe!" he called as he went on in.

He was stepping from the saddle before Pleasants showed himself again, and before two blanket-shrouded figures, Harry and Ben, roused themselves off near the ruin of the tent, got up, and came over to the fire to stare sleepily at him.

"What's on your mind?" Pleasants wanted to know.

"Hear you had yourselves some callers tonight," Crowe smugly remarked, pointedly surveying the tent's charred remains.

Pleasants stared at him stonily a long moment. "How would you know that?"

A deep resentment still burned in the saloon man. Right now he saw Lute Pleasants as being responsible for all the troubles that had plagued him tonight. Without preliminary, and in a bitter voice, he told the Beavertail man what had happened at the Pat Hand. Pleasants listened without once interrupting, without in fact showing any emotion beyond a none-too-strict attention, until Crowe finished by testily stating: "So I figure you owe me around two hundred dollars. You can damn' well pay up or I'll . . ."

"Or you'll what?" Pleasants's tone was chill, challenging.

"Or I'll be down at the Springs come mornin' seein' Jim Echols."

Pleasants found something amusing in the words and he smiled, very faintly. "You will?" he drawled. "And how would you get there? Walk?"

The way Crowe's high indignation so suddenly vanished before a look of utter astonishment made Pleasants laugh raucously in genuine merriment. He caught the way the saloon man's glance shuttled to the roan in futile understanding. Then he was telling Harry and Ben: "Boys, take Phil across there and pour him some coffee. Then see if you can find him a blanket. He's spending the night with you. And I'm not."

Crowe dismally saw the completeness of the trap he'd ridden into even before Pleasants sauntered over to take the saddle from the roan, heave it aside, cinch another in its place, and afterward thrust a heavy rifle in the saddle's scabbard. The saloon man stood quite placidly as Ben Galt came alongside him and relieved him of his gun. Only when Galt took him by the arm and started leading him toward the fire did he recover from his chagrin enough to jerk his arm free and growl: "I can walk by myself."

He went to the fire and resignedly watched Pleasants climb astride his roan. He tried to think of something to say, but couldn't.

Ready to ride, Pleasants said: "Better keep him around till I get back." Then he reined away and up the draw.

Lute Pleasants hadn't yet decided exactly what

he was going to do for the rest of the night, except that he did know he wasn't going to ride straight home. First of all he felt the need of putting distance between him and the fence camp. He wanted to rid himself of the bad taste left by as deep a humiliation as he had ever suffered. For he and his crew had been caught completely flat-footed by those two rifles on the ridge.

His own rifle—the .45-75 he now carried on his saddle—had been leaning against the trunk of a pine barely thirty feet out from the fire, and he hadn't dared expose himself by running to get it. His men likewise hadn't relished making a dash to the tent for their weapons. So they had taken a thorough bullet whipping, and the tent and their supplies were gone.

Try as he would, Pleasants couldn't put down the conviction that Frank Rivers had been one of the two men on the ridge above the draw. Perhaps, he was thinking, Rivers might even have been the man he'd surprised down there at the corral. He was certain that the shooting up of his camp had not only been Rivers's way of evening the score for the beating his crew had given Fred Bond last evening but also a clever means of keeping him from interfering with the moving out of Anchor's herd.

It rankled deeply to think that Rivers had outwitted him, that he might have been spared the humiliation of lying there behind the windfall and watching his camp being shot to pieces, then set afire, had he only left the draw a few minutes earlier. If he'd had only a five-minute leeway, or even a two-minute one, things might have turned out far differently.

Gradually, as the minutes passed and the roan carried him on south between the moonlit hills, he managed to stop thinking of all that had gone wrong and to wonder how best he could use the remainder of the night. He disliked wasting this unlooked-for luck of having had a horse walk straight into his camp. Crowe's arrival had, after all, in some small measure soothed the frustration and helplessness that had gripped him over the past four hours.

He was superstitious enough to believe in luck. And, now that he'd had this bit of good to outweigh the bad of earlier, he tried to tell himself that perhaps things weren't as bad as they seemed.

In addition to having heard the sound of cattle in the distance back there after the two rifles on the ridge had gone silent, he now had Crowe's word for it that Anchor's herd was probably already on its way down the pass road. And, grudgingly, he had to face the fact that after his weeks of careful planning there was little or nothing he could do to stop Fred and Kate from driving their cattle straight down to the railroad.

Thinking ahead, he finally began to rationalize that it would be a fairly easy matter to pay Crowe the money to heal the man's injured pride and persuade him to finish the fence that would wire Anchor off in the hills. For the moment he had lost the advantage in his months-long gamble of humbling the Bonds. But there remained the matter of Owl Creek running low next spring and summer, of the new fences slowly strangling Anchor. He was, he convinced himself, perfectly content to wait another year if need be to see the final ruin of the brand.

That decided, he felt considerably better. And when he shortly cut the Summit track, sheer curiosity took him along it. Reaching the pass road at the end of another half hour, he took out his watch to see that it was just ten minutes short of 3:00 a.m. He headed down the road, taking his time, even almost beginning to enjoy the night.

Some time later he was roused from a light doze by hearing the bawling of cattle sounding from close ahead. He left the road immediately, circling through the low hills until, from behind the concealment of a rocky hogback flanking the road, the moonlight let him see the drag of Anchor's shipping herd lined out along the track and moving steadily down toward the low country.

"Better make the best of it," he muttered softly, dryly, before he went on.

He rode into Ute Springs with the coming dawn, with the light strong enough to let him read the time by the courthouse clock: 4:20.

A faint surprise lifted in him at seeing lamplight glowing in the windows of the restaurant two doors below the hotel, though, as he turned in at the rail there, he understood the reason for the place being open as he remembered having noticed men working at the loading pens along the narrow-gauge siding above town some minutes ago.

On entering the restaurant he found the place empty except for Lou White, the owner. He took a stool at the counter and ordered steak and potatoes, and coffee right away.

White promptly brought him a steaming cup of coffee. "Sure been a busy night."

"Yeah?" Pleasants remarked sleepily, yawning.

"Three freights they loaded. The crews come in about midnight to eat. Then the Baldrock stage hit town late and I had four meals to get in a rush. And just now along comes Jim Echols and that bird that was with poor Cauble when he cashed in. Man, if business keeps up like this, I'm going to be missin' . . . ."

"Who? Who was with Echols?" Pleasants cut in, all at once wide awake.

"That man Rivers. The one . . . ."

"Oh, Rivers." Pleasants didn't let the other finish in his eagerness to learn more, to find out why Rivers wasn't helping Anchor's crew work its herd. "What would those two be doing, prowling around this time of night?"

"Search me. But Jim looked solemn as a judge. I come right out and asked him why he was night owlin'. All he'd say was that he wouldn't know till he'd made a seven-mile ride, that maybe he was wastin' his time." The restaurant man turned away. "Didn't make much sense to me."

A sudden premonition laid a chill through Pleasants that instant, though the next he was shrugging it aside by telling himself that seven miles wasn't only the distance to Beavertail but also to several other places. Yet, as he thought of it, he couldn't recall any other ranch or settlement that lay at that exact distance from Ute Springs.

And there was a note of urgency as he called to White, now standing at the stove back along the counter: "Hurry it up with that steak, Lou. I've got to be moving on."

CHAPTER TWENTY-TWO

B eavertail's clutter of sheds and shanties, its open-sided barn and pens and corrals, looked shabby even in the bright freshness of this early morning, Frank thought. The house, except for a new porch, was badly weathered and missing patches of shingles on its steep-pitched roof. One of the bigger outbuildings, probably the wagon shed, was leaning so precariously to one side that two logs were propped against its overhanging wall to keep it shored upright.

Close behind Frank, Jim Echols clucked to his mare, bringing her up even with the buckskin. "First time I've laid eyes on this layout in years," he remarked, dryly adding: "It's run down some since old Ruthling owned it."

They had covered another hundred yards along the weed-grown road when the lawman abruptly announced: "There's Charlie, the cook. See him? Walkin' across to the house."

Frank had no sooner made out the man, walking toward the rear of the house from one of the outlying buildings, than Echols was telling him: "Suppose you hang back and keep an eye open while I make medicine with that China boy. From the look of it, no one else is around. But we want to be sure, and we don't want to be together."

They rode on in at a jog, the sheriff pulling ahead as Frank's restless glance roved the house's yard, then studied the barn, the five horses in the corral, and finally a long, low structure behind the house he supposed must be the bunkhouse. Two dogs were barking viciously and had run out to snap at the hind hoofs of Echols's horse until a call from the cook quieted them.

Shortly Frank rode in past the house and swung obliquely across to the log buildings, his senses very alert as he reined in on the buckskin and sat, warily eyeing his surroundings. One of the dogs came across and, growling, circled him, the hair on its back stiff.

Echols by now was out of the saddle and talking to the cook, the two of them standing on the path leading to the house's rear stoop. Frank, made nervous by the thought that someone might be looking at him over the sights of a rifle, put the buckskin into motion again and rode over to the door of the cabin.

Reaching out with a boot, he pushed the door open, then leaned down to peer inside. This was the bunkhouse. It was empty.

He glanced toward the house then to see that Echols and the cook had disappeared. His nerves still on edge, he rode slowly on around to the front of the house, warily eyeing each window as he passed it, wondering if he and the lawman had played their cards wrong in so openly riding straight in here.

Rounding the front corner of the house, he was at once struck by the incongruity of such an elaborate new porch decorating an otherwise plain, even shabby structure. The unpainted wood of the porch didn't appear to be quite new, and he rightly guessed that it had been built a year or two ago. Pleasants, it seemed, had started to repair the house and for some reason hadn't finished the job.

He stiffened instinctively at the grating sound made by the front door opening and tensed his right arm, lifting hand to the handle of his Colt. Then the tightness eased from his nerves as the door swung back and Jim Echols came out onto the porch.

The lawman shook his head. "We draw a blank. Red Majors was here an hour ago. Hoofed it across for horses, ate an early breakfast, and headed back for their camp. Charlie says Red's feet were so swole he couldn't get his boots off."

"What about the rifle?"

Once again Echols shook his head. "Half a dozen of 'em in there. Forty-Four-Forties and one Sharps."

"He could have the Forty-Five-Seventy-Five with him." Frank was feeling let-down, weary. "So now what?"

"That'll take some figurin'." Echols was standing there, looking around at the porch. He came out to the railing, ran a hand along the smooth wood, absent-mindedly fingered the fluted contours of one of the posts as he went on: "First off, we could get up there on the pass trail and have a look for the mate of that shell we found yesterday. Then we might swing over and take a gander at their camp. But of course Pleasants won't be . . ."

His words trailed off and he frowned in faint annoyance as he took in the way Frank's glance had strayed, studying the porch. "You listenin'?"

"What?" Frank's puzzled stare came around to him. "What was that? Didn't hear you."

"Never mind. We'll talk about it on the way out." Echols came down the steps now.

"Jim."

The lawman looked up as Frank spoke his name. Then Frank was drawling: "That's a fancy porch to be tacked onto a house like this. Wonder who built it?"

"How would I know?"

"Go ask Charlie, will you?"

Something in the cool, wary way Frank was eyeing him made Jim Echols attach more than usual significance to the words.

Then suddenly the lawman understood. He went up the four steps in two quick strides, crossed to the open door, and bawled: "Charlie!"

The cook's voice answered him from some-where at the back of the house and he called:

"Who put on this new porch for Pleasants? Enos Ford from town?

In several more moments Charlie appeared in the doorway, his pale saffron face wreathed in a smile. "Enos Ford no good. Sam, he did it. Sam Cauble. He one hell of fine carpenter."

Jim Echols turned slowly to stare at Frank, incredulity loosening every muscle of his hawkish face.

"Hear that?" he asked. "By God, you knew. You've found your lame carpenter."

"You're wrong," Frank told him. "I've found his partner."

CHAPTER TWENTY-THREE

S o you've finally tracked down your man."
Frank Rivers, roused from his preoccupation, glanced around as Jim Echols broke the long silence between them. "Maybe," he said.

"Only maybe? No, friend. It's a surer bet than that. Cauble was lame. Now we know he was a carpenter. Someone took a shot at you the other night. You found out Pleasants had seen you in Summit that same night." He nodded sagely. "It all adds up. Pleasants has got to be the sidewinder that put that buckshot into your father. So's he got to be the one that nearly beat the life out of Bill Echols. Which'll make it a damned pleasant chore for me to see him hang."

"You could be right. We'll see."

They had ridden these five miles from Beavertail with scarcely a word having passed between them, each having his private reasons for being awed by the unexpectedness of their discovery that lame Sam Cauble had built the new porch on Pleasants's run-down house. Now, riding up the pass trail with the line of the new fence already in sight in the upward distance, Frank was still finding it hard to take in the fact that his long hunt might actually be nearing its end.

Wanting to believe the lawman's pronouncement,

he still wasn't quite convinced. For the chain of circumstance that finally made it appear that Lute Pleasants might be the man he had been hunting all these months was too tenuous, too obscure to be grasped as a dead certainty.

"I've been rough as a cob on you," Echols bluntly said just now. "So here and now I take back everythin'. About you beatin' up Bill, about your tryin' to make the governor's pardon look good." A wry smile touched the sheriff's hawkish face "Guess you'd say I made a plain loco fool of myself."

"Which you had a right to, Jim. So let's forget it."

"I'll try, and much obliged."

They swung off to the south now and in twenty more minutes had rounded the end of the fence and were coming up the trail to the low bench where Frank had camped his first night in this country. It was hard for him to believe that that night was less than a week gone, and, as he rode up on the blackened ashes of his fire, he was thinking of that other early morning when Lute Pleasants had led his men up this same slope to where he and Kate waited with Sam Cauble's body roped to the gray's saddle.

"This is the place." He reined in close alongside the remains of the fire, and nodded up the trail. "Whoever it was took his shot from up there."

"We'll go have a look." Echols frowned

thoughtfully. "Since it'd rained up here all that day before, chances are the ground wasn't froze solid. We could be lucky enough to run across some tracks."

The lawman was right. For in five more minutes his methodical traversing of the slope above showed him something that made him call across to Frank: "Here we are. Come take a look!"

The tracks had been badly washed out by the melting snow. But tracks they were, unmistakably, the line of the deep indentations angling down across the slope from the higher margin of the pines to a point close alongside a thin-trunked aspen.

Both of them got down out of the saddle near the aspen, the sheriff opining: "If this was him and not somebody else, then he must've tied his jughead about here." He looked down the slope to the place where Frank had built his fire, once again guessing. "He wouldn't have had to move much closer to be sure of his shot." And he began peering at the ground, moving on around the aspen.

Frank worked the ground farther out from the tree. Three slow minutes passed, two more. Once Echols cursed disheartedly, said: "I could be wrong about this."

Hardly had the lawman spoken before Frank stepped on a hard object that grated metallically as his weight ground it into the gravelly soil. He looked down, saw the dull sheen of brass. He knew even before he dug the shell case from the dirt exactly what he had found. It was a .45-75.

He called Echols across. The lawman took one look at the shell and a bleakness settled over his thin face. "Why would he do it, kill his own foreman, his partner?"

"Let's go ask him."

The sheriff sighed, turned away, and was walking across to his horse when Frank called to him: "What say we split up? You hit the fence camp. I'll go back to Beavertail."

Echols stopped, looked around. "You got a hunch?"

At Frank's nod, the lawman said: "Then we'll both head back to the layout."

CHAPTER TWENTY-FOUR

The town road first crossed the Porcupine five miles to the north of the point where it left Squaw Creek and climbed the bluff to the bench. And it was there, as the shoes of Crowe's roan lifted booming echoes from the planks of the bridge, that Lute Pleasants encountered the unbelievable.

It made him catch his breath with a sharp grunt of incredulity, made him pull the horse to a stand, and stare, wide-eyed and disbelieving.

The channel of the creek, broad and rocky, had two days ago been filled bank to bank with the run-off. Now it was bare and almost dry, littered with débris. At its center flowed nothing but a shallow three-foot-wide rivulet. The deep pool a hundred yards above the bridge, where Pleasants had many times glimpsed trout half the length of his arm, had shallowed to knee depth.

His square face went slack, turned pale with shock as he halfway understood the meaning of what he was seeing. His fists knotted the reins with a vicious strength that cracked the dry, unoiled leather. And for once he forgot to curse as the dread meaning of what he was seeing struck home to him.

"But the dam couldn't . . ."

His words trailed off helplessly as he groped for some logical answer to what could have gone wrong. For an instant he halfway believed that the dam he and his crew had thrown up across the mouth of the Owl the other night might have shifted so as to block the Porcupine. But then he knew that this couldn't possibly have happened.

All at once a feeling akin to panic laid its hold on him. Last night he had been outwitted on one count. Perhaps this was the raw evidence of Anchor, of Rivers, having outwitted him on still another.

For one rational moment he considered the possibility that someone at Anchor had noticed a change in the flow of the Owl. At first he ridiculed the notion. But then, when he thought of the way the weather had worked against him, when he remembered how quickly the snow had gone, the idea did seem plausible. And finally he had to admit that anyone familiar with the way the Owl might act under such conditions could easily have noticed that the creek's level wasn't what it should have been.

He had gone that far in his reasoning when a sound—the faint and faraway ring of doubletree chains shuttling in across the early morning hush—intruded upon his furious and bewildered thoughts. He looked on out along the road and saw a team and wagon coming toward him a quarter of a mile distant.

The hunched-over figure on the wagon's seat he recognized as being unmistakably that of Charlie, his cook. With an unruly impatience he spurred the roan to a lope and went out the road with the sudden hope that the Chinaman might have the explanation of the Porcupine's strange behavior.

Charlie's two dogs saw him coming and began barking, running out to meet him. He cursed them to silence as he met them and shortly reined in alongside the wagon, asking without preliminary: "What the devil's happened to the creek?"

The Chinaman's round face betrayed as much surprise as it ever did. "What about creek, boss?"

"Hell, haven't you noticed? You crossed it back by the layout. It's down, way down."

Charlie shrugged. "Part time sleep. Dream of . . ."

"Forget that and quit talkin' like a damned Indian," Pleasants cut in. "Today isn't Saturday. Why're you headed to town?"

"No one to cook for. I go see Cousin Sam, get grub, be back by noon." Regarding Pleasants with a narrower glance, Charlie bluntly, unexpectedly asked: "You in trouble, boss?"

"What?" Suddenly Pleasants remembered Echols and Rivers, and the hot flare of a fresh alarm ran along his nerves as he warily countered: "Me in trouble? Why should I be?"

"Red say you and boys catch plenty hell at camp last night. This morning two men come look for you."

"Who?"

"The sheriff and a stranger."

Pleasants felt the Chinaman's shrewd glance probing at him, studying him, as he loftily asked: "What could Jim Echols want of me?"

"No say, boss. But he look through house. Then want to know about new porch."

"What about the porch?"

"He say did Enos Ford build it. I tell him no, that Sam damn' sight better carpenter than Ford."

Pleasants's instinct was to reach out with rein ends and slash at the cook's round, yellow face. Yet he managed to curb that reckless impulse and ask calmly, in apparent disinterest: "Why would Echols care who built it?"

"Search me, boss."

When Charlie didn't add to that, Pleasants put another seemingly innocent question: "They waiting for me at the layout?"

The Chinaman grunted a negative, adding briefly: "Head for hills when they pull out."

"That's all?"

Charlie nodded, and for a moment Pleasants sat quietly trying to unsnarl the implications to the damage the cook had done him in revealing to Echols and Rivers that lame Sam Cauble had been a carpenter.

He recalled all too vividly that Rivers's lawyer, at the trial four years back, had attached great importance to the authorities locating as a witness the carpenter who had been working on the Wells, Fargo shack in Peak City the week before the stage hold-up and the killing of George Rivers. Also he clearly remembered what a shock it had been to both himself and Sam to learn that the Ute Springs sheriff was a cousin of the stage's driver they had left lying maimed in the road that night.

The enormity of the Chinaman's unwitting betrayal of him finally struck home to Pleasants. Yet, as he felt a real and craven fear tighten inside him, he managed somehow to keep a rein on his unruly temper. It was, he saw instantly, important that Charlie's suspicions of him be lulled. He must play for time, time to think out what he was to do about Echols and Rivers.

And it was with a nicely feigned nonchalance that he told the cook: "Well, Echols'll probably be back if he wants to see me. While you're in town, see if the market's got any ducks. Mallards. Been a whole year since I tasted one."

Charlie dipped his head in assent, said—"So long."—and clucked his team into motion.

As he went away, Pleasants sat watching him, for a moment coolly thinking that it would be very easy to draw the big Winchester from its sheath and send a bullet into the cook's back. But then he understood that Charlie could do him more good than harm now, for he had quieted the man's suspicions.

He went on along the road still trying to fathom

exactly how much Frank Rivers and Jim Echols might have guessed of his past, or if in fact either of them was even interested in what or who he or Sam Cauble had been before coming to the Ute Springs country. For minutes at a time he would feel that gnawing fear working in him. Then for equally long periods he buoyed himself up by thinking that most probably neither man suspected him of anything.

Jim Echols's curiosity about the porch might have been a perfectly natural one. So might this low water in the creek be explained in a perfectly logical way.

By the time he came within sight of Beavertail, feeling the effects of his sleepless night, he had convinced himself that he had nothing to worry about. Jim Echols would certainly have betrayed it to Charlie had his visit been prompted by anything of a very serious nature, and the cook had given no indication whatsoever that that was the case, or that the lawman had been in a bad mood.

Trying to believe this, Pleasants nonetheless reined in on the roan alongside the backdrop of the creek willows at the foot of his long meadow and for five minutes studied the upcountry distance. He saw no rider moving along the trail or hill up there, saw no one in sight around his headquarters buildings. And presently he took the track leading to the layout.

Some minutes later he was tying Crowe's borrowed roan at the barn corral gate and surveying the yard and outbuildings with a wary, restless eye. He found nothing to alarm him and shortly walked on over to the house, entering it by way of the kitchen.

He had it in mind to start on up the Porcupine within the next few minutes and to ride the stream until he discovered what was blocking it. But for the moment he wanted to stretch his cramped muscles, to rest. He went to the stove and filled a mug with coffee from the big pot simmering on the stove. He found the remains of a peach pie in the bread cupboard, took it from the dish and across to the table, sitting on the table's edge as he ate it, meantime looking out the window that gave him a view of the hills off to the east.

Tired as he was, he felt on edge, jumpy. Much had happened last night and this morning to confound him. He felt insecure, as though unforeseen events were overtaking him, closing in on him. And it was typical of him, scorning as he did any weakness in anyone, that he now tried to shrug this feeling aside by telling himself: *Get a hold on your nerve, man! Nothing's gone so wrong.*

Hardly had he become aware of the thought than he was seeing something that made him stiffen, quickly leave the table, and hurry to the window to open it so as to see more clearly.

Now he could make out two riders coming down the road that twisted out of the higher hills to skirt the foot of the meadow, the road that led to Anchor. The pair of horsemen was still better than a mile distant, too far to be recognized, and for a moment he thought that they might be Harry and Ben.

But then he was able to make out the color of one of their animals. It was a buckskin. And instantly the wariness in him tightened, threatened to become panic.

He swung quickly from the window, ate the last of the piece of pie, and emptied his coffee into the slop pail. He had put the cup on the counter and turned to the door before a thought made him reach for the cup again, dip it into the fresh-water bucket, shake it dry, and return it to the cupboard.

Outside, he ran as far as the corner of the house before looking out toward the road again. The riders had dipped from sight behind a low rise, and with a grunt of thankfulness and relief he ran for the barn. There he uncinched the saddle, tossed it and the saddle blanket aside, and hurriedly opened the corral gate, turning the roan in with the three other animals in the pole enclosure. Then, bridle in hand and lugging saddle and blanket, he ran into the barn and back along its runway.

He hung the saddle from a peg alongside three others. For a moment he stood holding the

Winchester, wondering what to do with it. For he had it in mind to hide if Echols and Rivers rode in here, to let them look anywhere they wanted for him, and to leave no telltale sign that he had been here during the interval they had been gone.

Finally he decided it would be best to take the rifle with him. By the time he was outside again, he saw that Echols and Rivers were once more in sight, now riding the line of the rail fence at the foot of the meadow. Crouching low and moving slowly, he crossed a fifty-foot open space that separated the barn from the bunkhouse. Once behind the log building he ran to its far end. Then, by circling behind the mound of the adjacent root cellar, he gained the house's back stoop without once moving into Rivers's and Echols's line of vision.

He had plenty of time to pick his hiding place now, though, as he tried to think of the best one, his thoughts ran anything but a straight course. He thought of the attic, discarded that possibility because it would place him beyond hearing the lawman and Rivers, should they ride into the yard.

What he wanted was a place of concealment within hearing if they should happen to talk. Finally he thought of a place. He would crawl under the kitchen stoop.

All at once it occurred to him that all his precautions might be wasted, that perhaps the two were merely riding on past on their way back to town. So he moved over to the corner of the house, took off his wide hat, and looked out along the line of the twin tracks leading up across the meadow.

They were on their way in.

He wheeled back behind the house. Even though it would probably be another five minutes before they could reach the layout, he ran for the stoop, went to his knees close to the wall of the house, and, carefully holding aside a clump of weeds growing close to the edge of the stoop, went flat and wriggled in behind the weeds, then in under the floor of the porch, pulling the rifle after him.

His breathing was heavy and labored, as he rolled onto his side and laid the rifle in the dirt, aimed at the opening through which he had crawled.

CHAPTER TWENTY-FIVE

They were riding even with the house's weed-grown yard, the bunkhouse directly ahead of them, when Jim Echols announced: "Wagon's gone. So are the dogs. Charlie must've taken off for town."

Frank's restless glance had been shuttling nervously between the buildings, and now the hard alertness that had been in him eased slowly away before a settling disappointment as he drawled: "Bum guess on my part. But I keep asking myself why he'd stick around his camp once he got something to ride."

"So do I."

The lawman had reined in and Frank swung the buckskin around and joined him. For several moments they sat looking about them, Frank taking out his pipe, then deciding he didn't want a smoke, pocketing it again.

"He was deaf if he didn't hear that herd moving out last night right after Fred and I finished busting up his camp," he said presently.

"Now that he's got a way of getting around, it could be he went on down to town to see if he could stir up any trouble for Kate and Fred."

"Unh-uh. There's nothing he could do without showing his hand and having me on his neck. He's

229

lost that bet. Let's look around," Frank suggested impatiently.

"Look where?"

"In the house to begin with. The rifle could be there. You could've missed it."

With a shrug, Jim Echols led the way on to the rear of the house. They stepped down from their saddles near the kitchen stoop and, ground-haltering their animals, went on into the house.

Frank was unaccountably feeling on edge as he followed the lawman from the kitchen and across a narrow hallway into another room furnished with a bed, a roll-top desk, a deep barrel chair, a wardrobe, and a horsehair-upholstered sofa.

"Here's his hang-out." Echols motioned to the gun rack on the outside wall. "And there's his rifles. Forty-Four-Forties, except for that Sharps."

"Where else did you look?"

"Behind the desk, under the bed, in that clothes closet."

"What about the other rooms?"

"There are only two more. Up front. Both're closed off, empty. I looked 'em over."

"What about the attic?"

The sheriff shook his head. "We could climb up there and have a look-see, sure. But you're forgetting. He doesn't know we're looking for that Forty-Five-Seventy-Five. So why would he have hid it?"

Frank had to nod grudgingly at the soundness of

that reasoning, though it did little to quiet the let-down feeling that was now laying its hold on him. "So what do we do?" he asked in near irritation.

"Well, it's a cinch he hasn't been here." Echols led the way back into the kitchen and out onto the rear porch, Frank following and closing the door. "So we either head for his camp or back to town. I'd pick town between the two."

Shrugging, Frank stepped to the edge of the stoop. He was dissatisfied with the lawman's answer and drawled: "Suppose you leave me here. Just in case. Or," he pointedly added, glancing around at the other, "maybe you're not trusting me alone with him."

The sheriff laughed softly, dryly. "I'd thought of that. You'd have to give me your word you'd try to bring him in without putting a hole through him. But you won't get the chance. We've been here twice and drawn a blank. He's either still at his camp or in the Springs."

"I'd still like to stay put, Jim."

"Suit yourself." Echols walked out to his horse, Frank following. And after the sheriff had swung up into leather, he looked down to say seriously: "I mean that about giving me your word to bring him in all in one piece if you run into him."

"You have it."

"I could be wrong about this. He could turn up here. And with his crew. Suppose he does?"

"You say he won't."

The momentary concern that had shadowed the sheriff's hawkish face faded. "I still say he won't. If he was coming here, he's had a world of time to arrive. So you're wasting your time. Might as well sit out in the sun and catch up on your sleep."

"Maybe I will."

Echols lifted a hand then and took his horse on out past the house and along the track leading south. He was halfway down the meadow before he made up his mind to ride straight to town and forget the fence camp. For if Red Majors had been here something like three hours ago, if he had gone back to the camp with horses, Pleasants would no longer be up in the hills. Since he hadn't come home, there was logically only one other place to look for him.

In a way, the lawman was relieved at not having Frank with him. On the way down from the pass trail he had realized that Frank, having wasted better than four years of his life on Pleasants's account, might well take matters in his own hands if he encountered the man. And had Frank done so, Echols could in no way have blamed him, for it was obvious that those four years had brought him much humiliation and bitterness, that a final settling of his reckoning against Pleasants was due him.

Yet Jim Echols was a lawman and a strict one, and, though he had a score of his own to settle with Pleasants for Bill Echols, he would see the law take the final accounting. He hadn't a shred of doubt but what he had the proof that would hang Lute Pleasants.

So now that he was alone, now that Frank was out of the way, his mind was more at ease. He would find Pleasants, make his arrest.

Leaving Beavertail's south fence behind him, he touched the horse with spur, going out along the bench road at an easy lope, anxious now to get to town and get on with this far from unpleasant chore. He would enjoy this arrest far more than any he had ever made.

Presently, when he crossed the upper bridge over the Porcupine and noticed the shallowness of the stream, he enjoyed a good laugh on wondering if Pleasants yet knew that his dream of ditching Beavertail's big meadow had dried up and blown away as surely as though a drought had hit the range.

Thinking of Frank Rivers, of all that had happened since the first day he had laid eyes on him, and particularly of all Frank had done for Kate and Fred, he wondered if he had ever so misjudged a man, or grown to trust and respect one more. There was a quiet sureness about Rivers, a capacity for facing down trouble, rarely found in so young a man. Frank had, he knew, been aged far beyond his years by more trouble and frustration than the average man found in a lifetime, and it left Echols a little awed to think that he had found not the slightest trace of bitterness in him. Frank Rivers was as good as they came.

He was shortly jerked from his ruminations at seeing a rider coming toward him up the road. For an instant he supposed that this must be Lute Pleasants, and his nerves drew wire-taut. But then the slightness of the figure told him he was mistaken, and in another half a minute he recognized Kate Bond astride her sorrel. Her animal was at a slow walk, and, as he came in on her, he could see that her shoulders sagged, that her head was lowered. For a moment a strong alarm ran through him. But then as the gap between them narrowed, he suddenly understood. Kate was dozing. The night she had spent in the saddle was taking its toll.

He had swung out and was turning his horse, about to fall in beside her, when she gave a start, lifted her head, and saw who it was. A tired smile wreathed her face and she spoke his name.

"Tuckered out?" he asked as she pulled the sorrel to a stand beside him.

"A little, Jim. But it was worth it." With an abrupt frown she asked: "Where's Frank? I met Lute's cook back there this side of town. He said you and Frank had been to Beavertail, looking for Lute."

Echols nodded. "Friend Pleasants wasn't there. Frank's still at the layout, waitin' for him. I decided it was a waste of time, that Pleasants was probably in town. So we parted company."

Kate's eyes came wider open in strong alarm. "But he isn't in town, Jim. The cook told me he'd met him here on the road. He was headed home."

"What!"

The lawman's single word was spoken sharply as a strong foreboding tightened every muscle in him.

"It's what Charlie told me. He wouldn't have any reason to lie."

Jim Echols knotted his right fist and hit the swell of his saddle a solid blow, swearing softly as he glanced back up the road. Then, lifting boots outward, ready to spur his horse to a run, he breathed prayerfully: "Let's hope it's not too late."

Before Kate quite grasped his meaning, he had thrown home the spurs and was running his horse back up the road.

CHAPTER TWENTY-SIX

F rank stood in front of the bunkhouse, watching Jim Echols until the lawman rode around the bend in the road that put him out of sight behind the creek willows beyond Beavertail's meadow fence. Then, trying to shrug aside the thought that perhaps he had after all made a mistake in not going to town with the lawman, he sauntered on down past the near end of the barn to the corral and climbed up to sit its top pole and lean back against the gatepost.

From here he could scan the hills that climbed to the east, he could watch both lower and upper reaches of the road. And as his glance idly studied the road, he was still wondering if his instinct had been wrong in making him think that Lute Pleasants would sooner or later ride in here. It was, he decided finally, a toss-up as to whether he or the sheriff had made the right guess.

The sun, well above the snowy peaks of the Bear Claws, had burned the night's chill out of the new day. He was tired and drowsy, beginning to feel the effects of the long hours he had spent in the saddle these past two days and nights as he took his pipe from his pocket, filled and lighted it, relishing the taste of the tobacco.

Once again it struck him that he might have used

bad judgment in not going with Jim Echols. It was galling to think that after all these months of hunting Pleasants he should miss the final showdown with the man even though that should turn out to be nothing more than seeing him put under arrest and locked in a cell of the Ute Springs jail.

Looking out across the corral, his idle glance examined the four animals standing hipshot beyond the water trough, tails lazily switching against the torment of the flies. One was a brown gelding, two were mares—a sorrel and a claybank, and the fourth a roan horse. The roan looked older than the other three and wore a strange brand faintly resembling the shape of a bird. It stood head down, dozing, the damp splotch left by a saddle blanket showing along its bony back and barrel.

All at once that dark marking on the roan took on meaning. And instantly Frank was thinking back, trying to remember how many animals he had seen in the corral on his and Echols's first ride in here right after dawn.

There had been five. He was certain of his count. Yet Charlie had taken the wagon to town, which meant he was using a team.

Unless someone had ridden in here while he and the lawman had been up the pass trail, there should be but three animals in the corral right now, not four.

Quickly he speculated upon the possibility that the roan's owner might have left in the wagon with the cook. Then, knowing the ways of horsemen, he rejected that explanation with the certainty that any man who had ridden a horse in here would be leaving by no other way than astride a saddle.

Suddenly and with absolute conviction he knew that he wasn't alone on the layout. Just as surely, and for no rational reason, he was positive that the man who had ridden the roan in here must be Lute Pleasants.

For a nearly overpowering moment he almost gave way to the wild urge to vault down into the corral and make a dash for the barn's side door, to do anything but sit here in the open. Pleasants had tried to kill him once; he might try again, if given the chance. But then as the seconds dragged on and no sound broke the morning stillness, he realized that by making any sudden move he would only be inviting Pleasants to cut him down, if in fact his hunch was right that the man right now might be watching him.

"Better think this out," he breathed softly aloud.

As quickly as that small panic had hit him, it subsided until shortly he was calm once more. He understood first of all that he couldn't simply sit here waiting for something to happen. Instead, he must somehow force Pleasants's hand. Or, if he was mistaken in his reasoning that the man had been the rider of the roan, he must prove himself wrong.

He eased around now and faced the house, reaching over to knock the tobacco from his pipe against the gatepost. Pocketing the briar, he glanced toward the house, studying first the side windows, then the rear.

The kitchen door was standing open. He had closed it on leaving the house with Jim Echols. Someone had gone into the house while he had been sitting here.

That someone was probably right now staring at him from the open kitchen window. He flinched momentarily as the realization struck home to him, then all at once that familiar prison-bred feeling of fatalism settled through him and he was ignoring the threat of the open window and thinking out what he was to do.

In several more seconds he eased down to the ground and, thrusting hands in pockets, sauntered obliquely over toward the front of the house. He passed a low-growing bush that screened him from the house and felt the strong urge to go belly down behind it, draw the .44, and wait this out, forcing whoever was in the house to make the next move. But then he realized that the bush would afford him no protection at all if the roan's rider chose to open up with a rifle.

So he went on at that same slow walk. And presently, as he rounded the house's front corner and could no longer see the side yard, a long sigh of relief escaped him.

He was shortly climbing the porch steps, letting the heels of his boots strike the wood so as to make each stride plainly audible if anyone was listening inside the house. He was acutely aware of the house's two front windows, of the possibility of someone inside watching him, and, as he crossed the porch, he whistled softly in hopes that he might appear to be doing nothing but killing time.

But then, as he reached out for the door's knob, his manner underwent a quick change. His tall frame tensed, his right hand came up to lift the .44 free of holster. In one lithe motion he pushed the door open, leveled the Colt, and eased quickly in through the doorway.

He was closing the door behind him with a sweep of the arm when he caught a blur of motion at the limit of his vision to his right side. He had barely begun to wheel in that direction when the vicious downswinging blow of some hard object struck him between neck and right shoulder.

The .44 flew from his grasp and spun to the floor as he was driven to his knees. He cried out hoarsely at the fierce knifing of pain in the shoulder as he instinctively reached down with right hand to break his fall, as the arm buckled and he fell against the wall of the hallway. Then he was lying there, looking up at Lute Pleasants, at the barrel of the big Winchester the man had used in clubbing him.

Pleasants's square face was set stonily as he lined the rifle at Frank, saying tersely: "On your feet, Rivers."

Over the pain that left him weak and breathless, Frank weighed his chances on swinging his legs and trying to use his spurs against the man's shins before the other could use his weapon. But then Pleasants backed away as though reading his thoughts, saying: "Move, damn you!"

Frank rolled onto his left side and pushed up to his knees, then came unsteadily erect, his aching left arm hanging uselessly at his side.

"All the way back," Pleasants told him, jamming the rifle's muzzle against his spine and pushing him so hard that he nearly lost his balance.

At the end of the hallway, Pleasants said—"Turn left."—and Frank led the way into the man's bedroom and office. "Sit down. Over there in the corner."

On his way across the room the toe of Frank's right boot caught in a hole in the worn rug, tripping him so that he halfway fell onto the horsehair-upholstered sofa in the back corner. That ungainly movement jarred his aching shoulder savagely, yet even over the pain he felt the arm move freely and with a vast relief knew that his collar bone wasn't broken.

Pleasants was watching him closely, his face

expressionless, his dark eyes bright with malice. "Hope I crippled you for good," he said tonelessly.

Frank leaned forward on the sofa, letting his aching arm hang straight as he rested his head against his other hand, trying to put down the nausea brought on by the pain. And in another moment Pleasants was gruffly asking: "So friend Echols is looking for me? Why?"

Frank tried to ignore his aching shoulder, tried to think of some innocuous answer he could give that would throw Pleasants off his guard. But then he understood that the man had probably overheard part, if not all, of his and Jim Echols's conversation here in the house and out in the yard.

Here was the man who had killed George Rivers and Sam Cauble, who had shot both of them down in cold blood. Here was a man who probably wouldn't hesitate to kill still a third time if he thought he was being deceived or tricked in any way.

In spite of that realization, all of Frank's long-nurtured contempt and loathing for his father's killer rose up in him now so that he answered bluntly: "He's going to lock you up, have you tried, and see you hang."

Strangely Pleasants's only visible reaction was a near-polite arching of his brows. "So you both know?" he asked.

Frank lifted his head and stared dully across at

the Beavertail man. "What you did to my father and Cauble? Yes, we know."

A faint glint of amusement touched Pleasants's glance. "It means I've got to plant you under the sod somewhere up in the hills, then get clear of the country."

Frank still didn't say anything, whereupon Pleasants coolly remarked: "Why I didn't use another bullet on you that night when you were with Cauble is something I'll never understand. Or," he added, "why I didn't use another on you the other night off there by Sawmill Ridge."

"Neither will I," Frank told him. "Because now you don't have a prayer of getting clear."

"No?" Pleasants laughed softly in real amusement. "Think again. By the time Echols gets back here the place'll be empty. You and me'll be long gone. There's a hundred ways a man can get out of these hills without being seen. I've made it a point to learn a few."

Frank was momentarily struck by the thought that Lute Pleasants was a different man today than the one he had been that early morning up the pass trail, and later in the sheriff's office in the courthouse. That day Pleasants had been unsure of himself, his truculent manner had seemed to be the cloak for some indefinable uncertainty and insecurity in his make-up. Yet this morning his every word and gesture were strongly positive, as though he had thrown aside all pretense and didn't in the slightest care that he was letting someone see his cold and brutal nature.

Just now the man moved over alongside his desk, leaned his rifle against the wall, and drew the .45 Colt from his holster. Letting the weapon hang at his side, he peered across at Frank, who was sitting with head hanging, gingerly rubbing his aching shoulder.

"What did Anchor do to the creek?" he asked.

Frank looked up at him. "We caved in the rim up by the forks. A train load of Giant powder couldn't blow that slide loose."

For the first time Pleasants seemed to lose grip of his cool and sure manner. His face flushed and, very softly, he drawled: "You've cost me a lot, Rivers. Too much. I've heard it said that a man with a bullet through the guts takes a long time dying. Tonight I aim to find out for sure."

Frank was feeling steadier with each passing second as the throbbing in his shoulder began easing away. Yet he saw it as being very important that Pleasants shouldn't know this. And now, as the other's belittling glance remained fixed on him, he lay back against the sofa, closing his eyes, and letting his big frame go loose, saying nothing.

Pleasants regarded him closely and in strong irritation a long moment, finally remarking: "At least Sam and I had a good ride while it lasted. Thanks to you. How'd you like the way we left you holding the sack up there at Peak City?"

Frank opened his eyes to meet the other's gloating stare. About to answer, he thought better of it, closed his eyes again, and, groaning softly, reached up once more to clench his bad shoulder.

With a shrug of disgust, Pleasants turned across the room and knelt in front of the big walnut wardrobe. He laid his gun on the floor nearby and, moving the rug aside, pulled the heavy wardrobe out from the wall.

Frank opened his eyes at the scraping of the heavy piece of furniture across the boards. Pleasants's back was halfway turned to him, and he was noticing the turned-back rug when all at once the man looked around and, with a spare smile, asked: "Know what I got hid back here?"

At Frank's feeble shake of the head, he said: "All I've saved these four years. And all Sam cached away. The poor souse never knew I was onto where he'd hid his share. Together they'll come close to eight thousand."

He bent forward and reached in behind the wardrobe, his back turned to Frank. Very slowly, very quietly, Frank nudged the rug's edge directly below him with the toe of his left boot. He felt the rug curl back. And suddenly in one swift, sure movement he reached down and caught a hold on the rug with both hands.

Pleasants heard the sofa's springs squeak. He looked around the instant Frank lunged erect, pulling the rug with him.

The Beavertail man made a frantic stab trying to reach for his Colt. His hand never completed its snatching motion. For all at once the rug was pulled from under his knees and he sprawled sideward, his shoulder smashing hard into the corner of the wardrobe.

Frank dived headlong at the man, grunting against the pain in his shoulder. Quick as he moved, Pleasants was quicker, rolling out of his way, lunging erect.

Pleasants saw Frank reaching for the Colt and frantically thrust out a boot, kicking the weapon under the wardrobe. Before he could draw his foot back, Frank snatched a hold on his boot, twisted it. Pleasants cried out in agony, fell to his knees. The next instant Frank's driving weight smashed into him from the side and his head was tilted hard around from a glancing blow alongside the jaw.

He rolled away, and then came erect the same instant, Pleasants swinging a vicious blow that caught Frank in the chest and drove him off balance, throwing him back hard against the wardrobe. Frank gasped for breath as Pleasants came at him. He lifted a boot, struck the other on the thigh, and turned him partway around so that he staggered into the doorway, jolting hard against the far side of the door frame.

Before Pleasants could push himself upright, Frank hit him a full blow in the face that turned him out through the door with such force that his heavy frame crashed against the far wall of the hallway. Blood streaked the man's face as he wheeled in through the kitchen door, then faced around as Frank came at him again.

Frank lifted both arms as Pleasants swung savagely at his face. He caught the blow on his right upper arm, wincing at the pain that lanced all the way up into his throbbing shoulder. He struck out with his left, hit Pleasants in the neck, and an instant later reeled back from a wicked smash at his left temple.

There was a split second when, his sense numbed, he knew that Pleasants could have decided this. But instead of coming at him, the man wheeled back around the kitchen table toward the outside door. And suddenly, exultantly Frank realized that this killer was afraid of him.

He lunged awkwardly toward the table, caught a hold on its edge, and upended it. One of the table's arcing legs tripped Pleasants and sent him jarring heavily to the floor in an ungainly fall that made him skid hard against the wall. And as Frank stepped around the capsized table and came at him, he threw his legs around, managed to stagger halfway erect, and frantically pulled himself out through the doorway and onto the rear porch.

Pleasants seemed to sense then that be would have no chance to make a run for it. For out there he turned, spread his boots wide, and brought up his guard, his eyes wide with shock and fright.

And before Frank had quite stepped out of the door, the man swung both fists at him, trying desperately to hit him in the face.

Frank instinctively hunched over. Pleasants missed with his left, but hit him on the top of his head with such a vicious, full right that he was momentarily stunned.

But Frank's weight was driving forward and the next instant he was close enough to reach out and throw both arms about Pleasants's waist. The man tried to knee him in the groin but lost his balance. Then they were falling outward and off the stoop.

Pleasants managed somehow to throw his weight around at the last instant so that Frank took the full impact of the fall on his bad shoulder. A wave of weakness came with the pain, and Frank lost his hold.

The Beavertail man pushed up, rolled almost out of reach, and was coming to his knees when, from somewhere out of the dim past, the memory of such a situation as this flashed across Frank's befuddled senses. It took every ounce of strength in him then to lift his legs, wriggle part way around, and straighten them. His boots caught Pleasants fully in the chest, threw him over backward.

As the other went sprawling, Frank came unsteadily to his feet. He stepped over and, as Pleasants tried to lunge erect, threw all the waning strength of his tall frame behind a hard left uppercut that caught the other on the ear and staggered him. Then, as Pleasants was groggily lifting his arms, Frank stepped in and swung a full, arcing blow that caught him on the hinge of the jaw.

Pleasants's heavy body stiffened. He was rigid, straight as a plank, as he fell face down into the dirt. He lay there without moving, groaning softly at each gasping breath. And Frank stood looking down at him, feeling so absolutely spent that he had to spread his boots wide to keep standing.

From somewhere out of the near distance Frank all at once caught the steady hoof drum of running horses. A surge of alarm coursed through him, making him step on out until he could see around the corner of the house and out the track leading up across the meadow.

Two riders were on their way in, their horses at a hard run. Frank thought of the rifle in Pleasants's bedroom, and of his own .44 lying somewhere near the head of the hallway.

He had swung around, ready to run for the kitchen door, when something faintly familiar about the look of one of the riders made him step out and peer toward the meadow again.

He recognized the rider on the left as being Jim Echols. And, in several more seconds, he knew that the other was Kate.

With a sigh of thankfulness he strode on back and past Pleasants to the well house. He had drawn a partly full bucket of water and was dumping it over his head when Kate and Jim Echols rode into the yard.

CHAPTER TWENTY-SEVEN

The last light was going out of the day as Frank walked up from Anchor's bunkhouse toward the lights in the two windows of the house's kitchen wing.

His six solid hours of sleep had left him feeling groggy but no longer so bone-weary as he had been as he fell onto his bunk at midday. He was stiff and sore, his right shoulder was tender to the touch. But as he breathed deeply of the pine-scented chill air he wondered when he had ever felt so buoyed up, so at peace with himself. This had been a day to remember.

He was coming in on the two tall spruce trees at the yard's edge when a shape moved out of the shadows toward him. His pulse quickened at recognizing Kate. Then the next moment she was asking: "Get a good rest?"

"Never better. How about you?"

"I slept like a rock." She stopped within arm's reach of him and he could make out the beauty of her smile then as she asked: "Does any of this seem quite real to you, Frank? Can you realize it's over?"

"It is a little hard to believe," he told her in all honesty.

"Frank, there's something I . . ." Kate was looking up at him intently as she spoke, as her

251

words broke off. And over the moment she hesitated, he knew instinctively that what she was to say was to be important to them both. Then she was telling him: "This morning, while you and Jim and the doctor were at the jail with Lute, Fred and I had a talk. We . . . we both want you to stay on. We don't want you to leave."

A feeling of awkwardness instantly laid its hold on Frank, so that he said the first thing that came to mind. "That's good of you. But this outfit doesn't need more than two men to work it over the winter. So . . ."

"So if you'd waited to ride up here with me at noon, I could have told you that Fred and I decided we'd try and buy the Beavertail. Which means that we'll need help, Frank."

He couldn't quite analyze the feeling that rose in him then, the delight and sheer happiness that made his voice unsteady as he quietly drawled: "That changes things, doesn't it?"

"It does." Impulsively she reached out and took his arm, pulling him gently toward the house. And there was a richness, a hint of strong emotion in her voice as she said: "Let's talk it over. Supper's waiting."

As they walked toward the house, Kate close beside him and the touch of her hand on his arm, Frank Rivers knew that he was leaving all the bitterness and heartache of the past behind him. The days to come would be full of a bright promise.

ABOUT THE AUTHOR

Peter Dawson is the *nom de plume* used by Jonathan Hurff Glidden. He was born in Kewanee, Illinois, and was graduated from the University of Illinois with a degree in English literature. In his career as a Western writer he published sixteen Western novels and wrote over 120 Western short novels and short stories for the magazine market. From the beginning he was a dedicated craftsman who revised and polished his fiction until it shone as a fine gem. His Peter Dawson novels are noted for their adept plotting, interesting and well-developed characters, their authentically researched historical backgrounds, and his stylistic flair. During the Second World War, Glidden served with the U.S. Strategic and Tactical Air Force in the United Kingdom. Later in 1950 he served for a time as Assistant to Chief of Station in Germany. After the war, his novels were frequently serialized in *The Saturday Evening Post*. Peter Dawson titles such as *Royal Gorge* and *Ruler of the Range* are generally conceded to be among his best titles, although he was an extremely consistent writer, and virtually all his fiction has retained its classic stature among readers of all generations. One of Jon Glidden's finest techniques was his ability, after the fashion of Dickens and Tolstoy, to tell his stories via a series of dramatic vignettes which focus on a wide assortment of different characters, all tending to develop their own lives, situations, and predicaments, while at the same time propelling the general plot of the story toward a suspenseful conclusion. He was no less gifted as a master of the short novel and short story. *Dark Riders of Doom* (Five Star Westerns, 1996) was the first collection of his Western short novels and stories to be published.